FOURTEEN STORIES HIGH

EDITED BY DAVID HELWIG
AND TOM MARSHALL

Library of Congress Catalogue Card No. 73–157710
ISBN 0 88750 046 3 (hardcover)
ISBN 0 88750 047 1 (softcover)
Cover by Ted Harrison
Printed in Hong Kong by Serasia Limited
PUBLISHED IN CANADA BY OBERON PRESS

CONTENTS

INTRODUCTION

Since the nineteenth century, the short story has been the
creature of the periodicals, but recently magazines,
especially in Canada, have been losing interest in fiction.
Chatelaine is the only commercial Canadian magazine that
still offers a place for short fiction. Otherwise the story
writer can look to a handful of American magazines, the
literary magazines and CBC *Anthology*.

Fourteen Stories High was begun in the belief that
Canadian writers were producing fine stories that should
be available to the general reader; and in the faith that
if it were easier to reach readers more and better stories
would be written. A second collection of new stories will
be published by Oberon Press next year, and the editors
and publishers hope that the collection will become an
annual affair.

It has from the first been part of our intention to
present a variety of fictional modes. Most previous
anthologies of Canadian stories have highlighted only one,
the naturalistic. There are no doubt good historical reasons
why Canadian writers – in this collection, for example,
Hugh Garner, Norman Levine, George Bowering, Alden
Nowlan, Douglas Spettigue and Don Bailey – have
worked so well (and, to be just, so variously) within this
mode. But it is no longer the only way in which Canadians
may wish to express the felt truth of their lives.

Thus Gwendolyn MacEwen explores the Canadian
reality in terms of myth as an expression of identity, and
Rudy Wiebe approaches an episode in Canadian history

from an unusual philosophical and perceptual angle. Andreas Schroeder makes of quite simple materials an existential myth, while Phyllis Gotlieb and Stephen Scobie project some of our present problems into the perhaps not-so-distant future. All retain a basic human concern.

It goes without saying that none of the fourteen writers can be categorized so easily as this. No one of them sounds like any other. Kent Thompson, Marian Engel and Nora Keeling, for example, each tell their story in a manner that suggests European influence. In some cases Borges, Barth and perhaps others may be felt as distant ancestors, but each tale is sharply individual. The house of Canadian fiction has many planes, perspectives and stories. Here are fourteen of them, the best Canadian stories of the year.

DAVID HELWIG/TOM MARSHALL

Note: contributions for the second volume (previously unpublished stories only) should be sent to the editors, Box 1061, Kingston, Ontario before 15 November, 1971.

A FEW NOTES FOR ORPHEUS

Don Bailey

I was sitting in my room when the phone rang.

"Hello."

"It's me," she said. Mother. I was almost glad to hear her. But something must be wrong. She never phoned me.

"Is something wrong?"

"Your father," she said. "The doctor called yesterday and told me."

"What! What did he tell you?" Why did she have to turn everything into one of those serial mysteries? Each episode yanked from her between commercials.

"I've been telling him for years," she said.

"Never mind that. What did the doctor say?"

"Cancer. It's in his lungs. I've been telling him for years but he'd never listen. Stubborn. Smoking his damn cigarettes like a train. I told him . . . . "

Her voice broke. She was crying. It made me angry to hear her crying for herself. She never once mentioned cigarettes that I could remember.

"Will you come up to the cottage this weekend?"

"Why? What's the point?"

"He's going to die!" she said, back to her favourite soap opera. "He's your father, Jake. You're his only son."

And you're his wife, I felt like saying; his only wife, but what was the point; it would be like taking away her bingo card with one number to go.

"Come," she said.

"All right. Tomorrow. I'll drive up in the afternoon."

"In the morning," she said. "Or tonight Jake. Come up tonight. I'm scared. When I'm alone with him I don't know what to say."

"I'll be up tomorrow."

"Early," she said.

"Yeah." And I hung up. It was crazy, her being scared after all these years of being alone with him. But it scared me too in a way. It was like suddenly now that he was going to die we had to face the fact that he was alive.

I sat staring at the telephone for a long time and thought about statues. I hated them. Statues were the way other people made you stand still. Like dying. People loved you, made you their hero and killed you so they could build a monument to their feelings. Statues. And now in my mother's mind I could see the old man turning to stone. She would buy the biggest and best headstone. Bingo! A perfect card. A prize.

I picked up the phone and called my wife.

"It's me," I said. My mother's son.

"You sound like the ghost of somebody I used to know . . . ."

The father, the son, the holy ghost. Yes the holy ghost was the rattling skeleton in my closet.

"I haven't got this month's cheque yet," she said.

"It's in the mail," I lied. I'd drunk it the weekend before with some girl from Baltimore who was in Toronto for a hairdresser's convention. You might say she clipped me, but I didn't mind, I needed a trim.

I like to make jokes to myself. It's a good cover for all the laughing I do.

"So how are things," she said. "Selling lots of cars?"

"Great, but I'm thinking of going into another field. Selling headstones."

"You make money at that?"

"People keep dying."

"I suppose . . . . "

I could see her, face pulled in like an accordion to squeeze her thoughts into a recognizable tune. Everything has to be familiar to her before she can accept it. I guess I never became familiar enough. And when I left she kept expecting me to come back. Like Eurydice waiting and

10

I didn't even look back.

"Is this a social call or what?" she said. "I haven't heard anything from you for months."

"Sort of business," I said. "How's the kid?"

"Great. She even mentioned you a couple of days ago; the man that used to live with us."

"I was wondering if it'd be okay for me to take her away for the weekend."

"Where?"

"Up to my parents' cottage."

"Since when did you get chummy with them?"

"Look Edith, it's just a thing. The old lady asked me up, the old man's sick and I said I'd come. I thought it'd be nice for the kid. Fresh air, swimming, the whole thing."

"What about me? I'm supposed to sit in this lousy sweat box while you and her go gallivanting off."

If she'd been in my room I would have punched her. It made me sick, the petty talk that led to this kind of thought. It was a way of chiselling at you, a re-forming. My wife, the reformer.

"She hasn't even met your father," she continued. "I can't understand why you'd want her to get involved with them now. You never did before. You hardly saw them yourself."

"Forget it then." I said. "I just thought she might enjoy the outing."

"I don't want to forget it, I want to know why all of a sudden you want to be nice to everybody. You know how often I've asked you to take her for a weekend so I could get away by myself, but you were always too busy. Now all of a sudden you're the good samaritan."

"Edith, my old man's sick. I want the kid to meet him at least once before he dies. At least once."

I was tired of this and sorry I had called. It had been a stupid idea and only proved how scared I was too. Frightened to go up there alone.

"Is he that bad?"

"Yeah."

"I never met him either," she said and began to cry. I began to wish that the hairdressers' convention hadn't

11

been the week before and that it would happen this weekend. Or that my phone was disconnected; I felt the same way from the calls being made to me and the ones I made too.

"I'm sorry," I said. And I was. I was sorry that that was all I could be. There was nothing I could change or would if I could, except maybe to never have had a phone installed.

"What time did you want her?" she asked.

"Whatever time's best for you."

"I'll send her over about ten," she said. "She can ride the streetcar by herself now."

She sounded proud. "That's great," I said. "I'll have her back Sunday after supper. Okay?"

"Take care of her."

"I will. Goodbye."

"Goodbye Jake."

I hung up and spent another long time staring at the phone. It was black like the night was becoming outside my windows. The phone could brighten up the night; one call to someone. A name somewhere in a directory.

I walked out to the balcony. The stars were like tiny animals' eyes. A coldness out there. "This is the winter of the world; and here we die." Did Shelley mean that? I'd have liked to have been on the moon with an endless supply of light bulbs; wire the moon to shine away the night.

I dreamed a while. Night dream of people I'd lost long ago in a daylight somewhere.

The old man was dying and I preferred to be seen in the dark. It was as though I was preparing myself for a sudden departure. Cutting myself off except for the phone. And telling myself I liked my privacy.

I went to bed early without even one drink.

A knock woke me. The room was full of light. A beam of dust particles formed a moving mural in one corner. In a way it was more of a picture than the posters I had pasted on the walls. Art should always be elusive. Somebody said that, I'm sure.

"Come in," I said. "It's not locked." I never lock the door. Locking anything defeats its own purpose.

12

"It's me," she said, and stood in the doorway with a brown shopping bag and a brown face split like a potato with a jagged grin.

"Com'on in," I said again. "Close the door."

She closed it and discreetly held her back to me while I fumbled around for my pants. They were on the floor and in a minute I was up and jamming the blankets from the studio couch into the closet.

"You look great," I said. "How's school?" Standard question.

"It's holidays," she said.

"Oh yeah. I forgot."

"You always forget," she said softly so I almost didn't hear her.

"You're starting to sound like your mother."

"I'm sorry. I didn't mean that. But you do forget. All the time when I see you, you always say you forgot this or you forgot that. All the time you say that."

It's true. And it's strange because I really want to be remembered. But not as a statue. I want to be remembered in an unclear way. Like a stranger that you see some night on the subway and never forget.

"Let's forget it," I said.

She laughed. "See!"

I laughed too. "I'm just lazy," I said.

She continued to laugh in the nervous way my wife has. An unnatural sound from a ten-year-old. But maybe not. I don't know any other ten-year-olds. Maybe they all end up sounding like that.

I shaved and came back to find her asleep. It frightened me.

"Hey, com'on sleepy-head, time to go. Didn't you get any sleep last night?"

"I couldn't," she said. "I was too excited."

At least she's still honest enough to admit what she feels.

"Let's go then. You got all your stuff?"

"Right here. I put my bathing-suit in too."

Because my living is made selling cars I always have a road-worthy vehicle at my disposal. My boss believes that as I zoom along the highway in one of his red convertibles, people will flag me down and make wild

13

offers to buy the thing from me. So far the only person who's flagged me down was a hitch-hiker headed for the east coast. Another dreamer. But still it's pleasant to have a nice car waiting for you at the curb. And the kid liked it.

"Can you put the top down?" she asked.

"Sure," I said.

The drive took less than two hours. Just over a hundred miles from Toronto. The old man had bought the cottage years back when I was still a kid and prices were on a level that only demanded a man's right arm stopping at the first joint. Now they wanted the shoulder and both legs.

With the top down it was difficult to talk and after a few distorted questions to each other that the wind blew around we gave up. When I pulled off the highway onto the dirt road that led to the lake she asked me something she seemed to have been saving for a long time.

"Do you have any girl friends?"

It startled me. Was she a spy? My wife liked to know things like that, but the kid had never sought information to take back with her before. Not that I could remember. Maybe I hadn't noticed. I didn't want to have to be cautious with her.

"Sometimes," I said.

"What do you mean?"

"I mean sometimes women are my friends but sometimes they won't leave me alone. You know what I mean?"

"Like mommy when she calls you?"

"Yeah, like that." But you're my friend, I wanted to say, but perhaps that wasn't true either. An infiltrator.

The old lady was sitting in a lawn chair when I pulled in the lane. Waiting. She got up slowly as though unwilling to admit we had arrived.

"I thought you'd be coming up on your own," she said when we got out.

"Thought I'd surprise you," I said. "You remember Bernice."

"I should say, my only grandchild. And how you've grown."

14

She didn't touch the kid. Standard policy. She hadn't seen her for over two years, since the separation, and she still didn't even put a hand out. Some families grow like trees, each separate but the branches touching from one to another and intertwining. Our family was like a series of telephone poles strung along a highway without even the wires to link us up. We were not a close family. I mean that as a kind of joke.

"What a lovely outfit," my mother said. "I'll bet your father got you that."

"My mother."

"Oh, wasn't that nice? And yellow too. You look so nice in yellow."

"Thank you," the kid said. I could tell it was killing her, this crap, and I was glad. All she had to do was one of those curtseys and the old lady would've been all over her, but the kid held back. No fancy dog tricks to get a bone and a pat on the head.

"Could you run along and play, Bernice? I want to talk to your daddy for a minute."

The kid fluttered around and took off into the trees behind the cottage; her yellow skirt like a wind-borne kite.

"What was the idea of bringing her up?"

"It was just an idea. You don't like it we can leave."

"You don't think I've got enough to worry about with him in that condition? And what's he going to think? He hasn't even met the girl."

"That's not my fault," I said. "And he can think what he wants. I figured it was time he met her. Where is he anyway?"

"Down at the dock," she said, and began to smile her secret scorn.

"What's he doing down there?"

The dirty pool look was there now. She was out to get him. She would have her revenge before she bought the statue. Her rule.

"When I told him you were coming, he decided you'd like to go fishing. He's down at the dock now getting the boat ready."

"That sounds like a hell of an idea. I haven't been

15

fishing for years. We can take the kid too. She's never been."

"Crazy foolishness, in his condition." She was disappointed. She wanted me to join her in lashing out at the crazy old bastard. She was right, he probably wasn't in any condition to fish, but maybe he was looking for revenge too. It was hard to say and I wondered where I'd fit in, if I did, and the kid too.

"He even took a case of beer down too," she said, as if this were some final proof of his unbalanced state.

"I'll go down and see him," I said. "Has he got the rods and stuff with him?"

"Everything. It's all gone down. He carried it all. If he'd've died on the path it's me that would've had to drag him back. He doesn't care. It's just too bad."

"Stop it, will you? Just leave the guy alone. We'll be back later."

She muttered something at my back that I didn't hear, but I'd heard it all before.

I found the kid sitting on a stump along the path to the lake. She faced the trail as though she'd been waiting. Sure I'd come. That felt nice for some reason.

"Is he really my grandfather?" she asked.

"Sure. My father, your grandfather."

She took my hand and hers was warm and wet and I moulded its gentle roughness like an autumn apple. She knew the gestures that lead me to standing still. For statue making. To become a hero. But it was only for today, I thought. I could afford it for one day at least.

"Mommy's father is dead," she said. "He was my grandfather too."

"I know."

"How come your father never came to see us. Mommy's did sometimes."

"He's pretty busy," I said. "I hardly ever see him myself."

"Like you," she said. "Always busy too."

"Not like that. I mean . . . . " I couldn't assemble the words to build the picture the way it really was. Maybe someday.

"He's been sick a lot," I said.

16

"Oh." It was a wounded sound. A moan. Orpheus looking back and regretting it in his throat.

We passed out of the trees and could see the water now. The sight, sheared from our full view by more trees, left the shape of an orchestra pit. It shone in the sun like a bluefuzz blanket. And the old man was there in front of us loading something in the boat.

"That's him," I said.

"I see. He's smaller than you."

She was right. I had always thought of him as being bigger, but he was tiny and shrivelled in an old-dog kind of way. I hadn't seen him in over two years and it was like I had forgotten what he looked like.

"This is a surprise," he said. "Who've we got here?"

"This is my daughter Bernice. This is my father, Bernice, your grandfather."

"Well," he said, and took her hand smoothly. They walked away, he holding her hand and talking. "I was just gettin' the boat ready to do a bit of fishin'. You ever been fishin'?"

She shook her head. The long brown strands of hair reflecting gold in the sharply focussed sun. Her mother's hair. It had reflected like that two summers ago in this very spot. Nothing changes.

"It okay to bring her along Jake?"

His tone was polite but we all knew the question had been settled. He was already helping her into the boat.

"Sure," I said. "You got an extra rod?"

"She can use mine."

He'd done it again. I stood there feeling awkward, the way I had so often in the past. Like I was a kid again and didn't know what to do with my hands or feet, or the words in my mouth.

"You comin' Jake?" He was behind the motor tugging at the cord, as thin as the cord himself and looking frail in a tough way with an old raggedy wine-coloured sweater dropping from his shoulders. So often in the past when he had offered things in that tone I'd refused. Now I jumped into the boat before he left without me.

He had the kid sitting across from him helping steer the boat as it plowed through the water making miniature

17

rainbows in the spray. He was talking to her but I couldn't make out the words above the sound of the engine.

Once he had taken me to a baseball game at Maple Leaf Stadium. In the eighth inning I had to go to the bathroom, and he didn't want to miss any of the game so he let me go by myself. I was seven or eight. I got lost and he didn't find me until an hour after the place was cleared out. He wasn't angry. Disappointed maybe. And I was ashamed. Always when I was around him I did things to make me ashamed.

The motor slowed, gurgled, stopped. He dropped the paint can full of stones he used for an anchor.

"Is this the place where you catch the fish?" the kid asked. She was excited now, on the brink of some new discovery. Animated face like her mother.

"This is it," he said, "but don't forget what I said, fish can hear, so you've gotta be real quiet."

She put her hand to her mouth and ssshed.

"Right," he said.

So easy for her to get his approval. Was it easier now than it had been for me? He baited the hook for her as she watched intently. He plunked the line in the water and looked up to see me watching him.

"I was just remembering the first time you showed me how to put a worm on a hook," I said. "You remember?"

He laughed drowsily and coughed quietly. He was a quiet man, I thought. A quiet, polite man. He was sitting four feet away dying the same way he had lived.

"You were worse than a girl," he said.

"Yeah," and I tried to smile politely too, but I had always resented that about him; his attitude to my . . . what did the old lady call it? My frailness.

"Sssh daddy, the fish'll hear," Bernice cautioned, her face serious.

The old man smiled. He had a way. Maybe I was jealous. I was a sickly kid, lousy at sports, anything physical, but he had a way of making it harder for me. Just stand there politely smiling at my attempts. He never laughed. Just that damn polite smile. And sometimes, now that I remembered, not even that. He wasn't always around when I tried my stunts; the day I finally made the

18

hockey team and actually scored a goal. The second-place medal for swimming. He was busy playing golf, a game he was so good at different people encouraged him to turn pro. That made me proud when I heard that. I had day-dreams of caddying for him in the big tournaments, but he just smiled his polite smile and said no.

I watched him put together a cigarette. He rolled his own and his hands moved quickly like a woman knitting.

"Nothin' bitin'," he said.

"No, not today by the look of it. Could be too hot. Maybe we should go in. The kid's got no hat, she might get sun-stroke."

"I'm okay daddy. This is fun."

She kept standing up when she thought she had a bite. It made me nervous but the old man was right beside her. She was okay. Just my nerves.

"A beer?" he said.

"Yeah. Okay." He handed me a bottle and it was warm in the clammy way of a fish. I drank it quickly. I like beer, it reminds me of my mother: from hand to mouth, that's the way she describes the way I live, from hand to mouth. The beer being lifted, sucked at, the liquid measuring out my life. Like Hemingway, I thought with a sudden fright. From hand to mouth; his hand taking the gun to his mouth because he had nothing left to say and no reason to go on living. His statue moulded and waiting for his death.

My trouble is I want to be remembered so much and yet I spend my time trying to forget. That's what my life is about these days; trying to forget. My wife. The kid. Mother. Everyone including the old man, and I never wanted to be spending this weekend with him in a boat supposedly fishing. I've dreaded the thought of such a weekend all my life.

"Surprised you're up this way," he said.

"Mom invited me."

"Probably told you about the business," he said.

So like him; business, his death.

"Yeah, she mentioned you weren't well."

"She gets excited."

Not like you with your polite smile.

19

"Daddy, you guys are gonna scare all the fish."

The old man puffed on his cigarette and grinned, his mouth unsealing like a steamed envelope. What was behind the flap? What songs had found their way out, or had any? Had the old man ever made music somewhere with someone? I'd have liked to have known. Somehow I felt it would make me feel better if he had. More hopeful. Something.

And suddenly the kid was standing, jerking forward like a Buddhist monk in prayer falling to his knees.

"There's something . . . " she yelled and splashed into the water.

It was a short distance to fall from her position at the back of the boat and I watched the bright yellow dress congeal into a dish rag. It was all so strange: once I had fallen off the end of the dock when I was five. I may even have done it on purpose and I kept my eyes open in the water as I sank and I saw the eerie arm of my father reach down and grab me. He used a fish gaff to hook me. I still have the scars on my shoulder. The proof. Of something.

The old man was right beside her. All he had to do was reach over the side and pull her in. It would be easy for him.

He yelled at me. Something was wrong. He never yelled. A quiet polite man.

"Get her Jake! Move, you stupid bugger!"

Me.

I plunged in. The water turned my clothes into a smothering blanket. It was cold. I couldn't see her. I had to go up. I couldn't breathe. I didn't want to drown. I didn't want to die. I really didn't.

Oh God! Everything was ending. God. God. God. Damn. And then I saw her. She was upside down, her dress over her head. She seemed to be spinning slowly and I grabbed a leg. I pawed upward with my hand, not knowing any longer that there was anything beyond. The surface was a spot in my mind that had receded to a soft blur. Like a memory of a long-ago pain.

But it was there waiting. I punched into the air, my arm clawing for something to hold but the boat was several yards away. I saw the old man still seated. He spotted me and leaned forward, yelled something and I was under again. I fought to turn the girl around. She was like a shot deer. Stiff feeling. Her head was up and I cupped her under the chin and swam back to the boat just the way I'd been taught in the Red Cross life-saving course. The old man hadn't been around when I got that certificate either.

He was waiting and held her arms while I crawled in the boat. Everything was clear now. Pull her aboard, put her on the bottom of the boat with his sweater under her head. Check her mouth for obstructions. Head to one side. Arms in position. Pushing down gently. Pulling back. Counting. And repeating the whole thing over and over again.

The old man watched. He rolled a cigarette and coughed politely several times. He didn't smile and I saw he was sweating.

She began to cough. And then she was sick. That was good. It was okay. She began to cry. And then louder, screaming. Shock. The old man handed me his sweater and I wrapped her in it. Soon it was reduced to a sob.

"Daddy, the fish tried to take me away."

"It's okay baby. Everything's okay. I've got you now."

And as suddenly as the tears had come, she fell asleep in my arms.

We sat there for a few minutes and then the old man spoke.

"I'm sorry Jake. I just didn't have the strength. She was right there but I didn't have the strength to get her. She could've drowned."

"She didn't," I said. "That's the main thing. Everything's all right now."

"We'd better go back," he said.

He turned and started the motor. The girl slept huddled against me, and I thought of the phone in my room, the receiver in its cradle. And I thought of all the nights when I had almost called so many people like the girl I was holding. After today I would have to begin to make some of those calls or have the phone removed. I wasn't sure why, but something had changed and I'd have to face it.

At the dock he helped me lift her out of the boat.

"Careful," I said.

"I'm fine now," he said. "Just sometimes my strength goes all out of me."

"You shouldn't've gone to all this trouble with the boat," I said.

He smiled. Polite again. We began walking back to the cottage, the girl asleep still in my arms.

"See Jake," he said, when we reached the trees, "I'm a selfish man."

"We all are," I said.

"Yeah, but with me it was different in some way. Sometimes I feel like I missed something. I always figured the most important thing to a man was his privacy. A man's got to have his privacy. I always lived that way Jake."

It may have been an explanation or even an apology but whatever it was, it was enough. He'd had his polite smile all his life and I had my telephone. You could hide behind either one or use it to reach out. I could learn a lot from the old man. If only he'd tell me. Maybe, though I had to ask. And maybe privacy was another way of saying lonely.

The old lady was waiting for us on the path. He walked straight toward her voice. I felt the pinch of her words and fell behind. The man walked straight ahead and didn't look back.

HOUSE OF THE WHALE

Gwendolyn MacEwen

Of course I was never a whale; I was an Eagle. This prison is a cage for the biggest bird of all. I'm waiting for them to work their justice, you see, and while I'm waiting I'm writing to you, Aaron, good friend, joker. The hours pass quickly here, strange to say; I have all kinds of diversions. The nice fat guard with the bulbous nose and the starfish wart at the tip often greets me as he makes his rounds. I make a point of waiting at the front of the cell when I know he's coming. And then there's Mario in the next cell who taps out fascinating rhythms at night with his finger-nails against the walls.

I don't have an eraser with me, Aaron, so any mistakes I make will have to stay as they are, and when the pencil wears down, that will be that.

I can't help thinking how young I still am—23. Twenty-three. Can I tell you about my life again? It was normal at first. I wrenched my mother's legs apart and tore out of her belly, trailing my sweet house of flesh behind me. I lay on a whaleskin blanket and watched the water; I sucked milk; I cried. I was wrapped up in thick bearskin in winter. I was bathed in the salt water of the sea. My mother was taller than all the mountains from where I lay.

There were the Ravens and the Eagles. You already know which I was. When I was old enough to take notice of things around me, I saw the half-mile line of our houses facing the waters of Hecate Strait. And I saw the severe line of the totems behind them, guarding the village,

23

facing the sea—some of them vertical graves for the dead chiefs of old. Some totems, even then, had fallen, but our Eagle still looked down on us from the top of the highest one, presiding over the angular boats on the beach, the rotting cedar dugouts and black poplar skiffs. (Someone ages before had suggested getting motors for them— the boats, that is—and the old men of the village almost died.)

I was turned over to my uncle's care after I passed infancy, and he spoke to me in the Skittegan tongue and told me tales in the big cedar-plank house. I've long since forgotten the language, you know that, but the stories remain with me, for stories are pictures, not words. I learned about the Raven, the Bear, the Salmon-Eater and the Volcano Woman—just as your children someday will learn all about Moses or Joshua or Christ.

I never knew my father; after planting me in my mother's belly he left to go and work in the Commercial Fisheries on the mainland. He forsook the wooden hooks and cuttlefish for the Canneries—who could blame him? Secretly, I admired him and all those who left the island to seek a fortune elsewhere, to hook Fate through the gills. But he never came back.

Our numbers had once been in the thousands but had dwindled to hundreds, My grandfather, who was very old, remembered the smallpox that once stripped the islands almost clean. He remembered how the chiefs of the people were made to work in the white man's industries with the other men of the tribe, regardless of their rank; he remembered how the last symbols of authority were taken away from the chiefs and *shamans*. A chief once asked the leader of the white men if he might be taken to *their* island, England, to speak with the great white princess, Victoria—but he was refused.

Sometimes I heard my grandfather cursing under his breath the Canneries and hop fields and apple orchards on the mainland. I think he secretly wished that the Sacred-One-Standing-and-Moving who reclined on a copper box supporting the pillar that held the world up would shift his position and let the whole damn mess fall down.

When I was young some of our people still carved argillite to earn extra money. It was a dying art even then, but the little slate figures always brought something on the commercial market. The Slatechuk quarry up Slatechuk creek was not far from Skidegate; and there was an almost inexhaustible supply of the beautiful black stone, which got shaped into the countless figures of our myths. I remember having seen Louis Collison, the last of the great carvers, when I was still a child. I watched his steady gnarled hands creating figures and animals even I didn't know about, and I used to imagine that there was another Louis Collison, a little man, who lived inside the argillite and worked it from the inside out.

(The fine line, Aaron, between what is living and what is dead . . . what do I mean, exactly? That party you took me to once in that rich lady's house where everyone was admiring her latest artistic acquisition— a *genuine Haida* argillite sculpture. It illustrated the myth of Rhpisunt, the woman who slept with a bear and later on bore cubs, and became the Bear Mother. Well, there were Rhpisunt and the bear screwing away in the black slate; Rhpisunt lay on her back, legs up, straddling the beast, her head thrown back and her jaws wide open with delight—and Mrs. What's-Her-Name kept babbling on and on about the "symbolic" meaning of the carving until I got mad and butted in and told her it was obviously a bear screwing a woman, nothing more, nothing less. She looked upset, and I was a little drunk and couldn't resist adding, "You see, I too am *genuine Haida.*" And as the party wore on I kept looking back at the elaborate mantelpiece and the cool little slate sculpture, and it was dead, Aaron, it had *died*—do you see?)

My mother wove baskets sometimes and each twist and knot in the straw was another year toward her death. And she sometimes lit the candlefish, the *oolakan* by night, and we sat around its light, the light of the sea, the light of its living flesh. Sometimes the old *shaman* would join us, with his dyed feathers and rattles, and do magic. I saw souls and spirits rising from his twisted pipe; I saw all he intended me to see, though most of the people left in the village laughed at him, secretly of course.

25

My grandfather was so well-versed in our legends and myths that he was always the man sought out by the myth-hunters—museum researchers and writers from the mainland—to give the Haida version of such-and-such a tale. My last memory of him, in fact, is of him leaning back in his chair and smoking his pipe ecstatically and telling the tale of Gunarh to the little portable tape-recorder that whirred beside him. Every researcher went away believing he alone had the authentic version of such-and-such a myth, straight from the Haida's mouth—but what none of them ever knew was that grandfather altered the tales with each re-telling. "It'll give them something to fight about in their books," he said. The older he got, the more he garbled the tales, shaking with wicked laughter in his big denim overalls when the little men with tape recorders and notebooks went away.

Does he think of me now, I wonder? Is he still alive, or is he lying in a little Skidegate grave after a good Christian burial—a picture of an eagle on the marble headstone as a last reminder of the totem of his people? Is he celebrating his last *potlache* before the gates of heaven; and has the *shaman* drummed his long dugout through waves of clouds? Are the *ceremonial* fires burning now, and is my grandfather throwing in his most precious possessions —his blue denim overalls, his pipe?

(Remember, Aaron, how amazed you were when I first told you about the *potlache*? "Why didn't the chiefs just *exhibit* their wealth?" you argued, and I told you they felt they could prove their wealth better by demonstrating how much of it they could *destroy*. Then you laughed, and said you thought the *potlache* had to be the most perfect parody of capitalism and consumer society you'd ever heard of. "What happened," you asked, "if a chief threw away everything he owned and ended up a poor man?" And I explained how there were ways of becoming rich again—for instance, the bankrupt chief could send some sort of gift to a rival chief, knowing that the returned favour had to be greater than the original one. It was always a matter of etiquette among our people to outdo another man's generosity.)

Anyway, I lie here and imagine grandfather cele-

26

brating a heavenly *potlache*—(heaven is the only place he'll ever celebrate it, for it was forbidden long ago by the government here on earth)—and the great Christian gates are opening for him now, and behind him the charred remains of his pipe and his blue denims bear witness to the last *potlache* of all.

Some of my childhood playmates were children of the white teacher and doctor of Skidegate, and I taught them how to play *Sin*, where you shuffle marked sticks under a mat and try to guess their positions. They got sunned up in summer until their skins were as copper as mine; we sat beneath the totems and compared our histories; we sat by the boats and argued about God. I read a lot; I think I must have read every book in the Mission School. By the time I was fifteen I'd been to the mainland twice and come back with blankets, potato money, and booze for the old *shaman*.

I began to long for the mainland, to see Vancouver, the forests of Sitka spruce in the north, mountains, railroads, lumber camps where Tsimsyan and Niskae workers felled trees and smashed pulp. My uncle had nothing to say when I announced that I was going to go and work at "the edge of the world"—but my grandfather put up a terrific fight, accusing me of wanting to desert my people for the white man's world, accusing my mother of having given birth to a feeble-spirited fool because on the day of my birth she accepted the white man's pain-killer and lay in "the sleep like death" when I came from her loins. And then he went into a long rambling tale of a day the white doctor invited the *shaman* in to witness his magic, and the *shaman* saw how everything in the doctor's room was magic white, to ward off evil spirits from sick flesh, and he saw many knives and prongs shining like the backs of salmon and laid out in neat rows on a white sheet; from this he understood that the ceremony wouldn't work unless the magical pattern of the instruments was perfect. Then the doctor put the sick man into the death-sleep, and the *shaman* meanwhile tried to slip the sick soul into his bone-box, but he couldn't because the doctor's magic was too powerful to be interfered with. It was only when the doctor laid out

27

exactly four knives and four prongs onto another white sheet, that the *shaman* realized the doctor had stolen the sacred number four from us to work his magic.

I worked north in a lumber camp for a while; we were clearing a patch of forest for an airplane base. In one year I don't know how many trees I killed—too many, and I found myself whispering "Sorry, tree" every time I felled another one. For *that* I should be in prison—wouldn't you think? Wasn't it worse to destroy all those trees than do what I did? Oh well, I can see you're laughing in your beer now, and I don't blame you. Anyway, I really wanted to tell you about Jake and the other guys in the bunkhouse, and what a great bunch they were. I learned a lot about girls and things from them, and since I didn't have any stories of my own like that to tell them, I told them the myth of Gunarh—you know the one; you said the first part of it is a lot like a Greek myth—and all the guys gathered round, and Jake's mouth was hanging open by the time I got to the part about Gunarh's wife eating nothing but the genitals of male seals . . . .

"Then she took a lover," I went on, "and her husband discovered her infidelity and made a plan."

"Yea, yea, go on, he made a *plan*!" gasped Jake.

"He—"

"SHADDUP YOU GUYS, I'M TRYING TO LISTEN!"

"When they were asleep after a hard night, the lover and the wife . . . "

"Hear that, guys—a HARD night!"

"Jake will ya SHADDUP!"

"—Gunarh came in and discovered them together. He killed the lover and cut off his head and his—"

"Jesus CHRIST!"

"Jake will ya SHADDUP!"

"—and put them on the table . . . . "

"Put *what* on the table?"

"It ain't the *head*, boys!"

"Jesus CHRIST!"

"So the next morning his wife found her lover gone, and she went to the table for breakfast—you remember what she usually ate—and instead of . . . "

"O no! I'm sick, you guys, I'm sick!"

"SHADDUP!"

"—well, she ate *them* instead."

"Jake, will ya lie down if you can't take it?"

I never did finish the story, because they went on and on all night about what Gunarh's wife ate for breakfast, and Jake kept waking up and swearing he was never going to listen to one of my stories again, because it was for sure all Indians had pretty dirty minds to think up things like that.

Almost before I knew it, my year was up and I was on a train heading for Vancouver; the raw gash I'd made in the forest fell back behind me.

At first I spent a week in Vancouver watching the people carry the city back and forth in little paper bags; I stayed in a strange room with a shape like a big creamy whale in the cracked plaster on the ceiling, and curtains coloured a kind of boxcar red which hung limply and never moved. I drank a lot and had some women and spent more money than I intended, and after standing three mornings in a row in a line-up in the Unemployment Office, I bumped into you, Aaron, remember, and that was the beginning of our friendship. You had a funny way of looking at a person a little off-centre, so I was always shuffling to the left to place myself in your line of focus. I can't remember exactly what we first talked about; all I know is, within an hour we'd decided to hitch-hike to Toronto, and that was that. At first I hesitated, until you turned to me, staring intently at my left ear, and said, "Lucas George, you don't want to go back to Skidegate, you're coming east." And it was that careless insight of yours that threw me. You always knew me well, my friend. You knew a lot, in fact—and sometimes I was sure you kept about 50% of your brain hidden because it complicated your life. You were always a little ahead of yourself—was that the reason for your nervousness, your impatience? You could always tell me what I was thinking, too. You told me I was naive and you liked me for that. You predicted horrible things for me, and you were right. You said my only

29

destiny was to lose myself, to become neither Indian nor white but a kind of grey nothing, floating between two worlds. Your voice was always sad when you spoke like that . . . .

Hey Aaron, do you still go through doors so quickly that no-one remembers seeing you open them first?

My grandfather's tales, if he's still alive, are growing taller in Skidegate. My mother's baskets, if she's still alive, are getting more and more complicated—and the salmon are skinnier every season. My time's running out, and I'd better finish this letter fast.

You were silent in B.C. but you talked all the way through Alberta and Saskatchewan; we slept through Manitoba and woke up in Ontario. The shadows of the totems followed me, growing longer as the days of my life grew longer. The yellow miles we covered were nothing, and time was even less.

"Lucas," you turned to me, "I forgot to tell you something. In B.C. you were still something. Here, you won't even exist. You'll live on the sweet circumference of things, looking into the centre; you'll be less than a shadow or a ghost. Thought you'd like to know."

"Thanks for nothing," I said. "Anyway, how do *you* know?"

"I live there too, on the circumference," you said.

"What do you do, exactly?"

"I'm an intellectual bum," you answered, "I do manual work to keep my body alive. Sometimes I work above the city, sometimes I work below the city, depending on the weather. Skyscrapers, ditches, subways, you name it, I'm there . . . . "

Aaron, I only have a minute left before they turn the lights out for the night. I wanted to ask you . . . .

Too late they're out

"Well," you said, the first day we were in the city, "Welcome to the House of the Whale, Lucas George."

"What do you mean?" I said.

"Didn't you tell me about Gunarh and how he went to the bottom of the sea to rescue his wife who was in the House of the Whale?"

"Yes, but—"

"Well, I'm telling you *this* is the House of the Whale, this city, this place. Ask me no questions and I'll tell you no lies. This. This is where you'll find your *psyche*."

"My *what*?"

"This is where you'll find what you're looking for."

"But, Aaron, I'm not looking for anything really!"

"Oh yes you are . . . . "

We stood looking at City Hall with its great curving mothering arms protecting a small concrete bubble between them. Behind us was Bay Street and I turned and let my eyes roll down the narrow canyon toward the lake. "That's the Wall Street of Toronto," you said. "Street of Money, Street of Walls. Don't worry about it; you'll never work there."

"So what's down there?" I asked, and you pointed a finger down the Street of Walls and said, "That's where the whales live, Lucas George. You know all about them, the submerged giants, the supernatural ones . . . . "

"The whales in our stories were gods," I protested. And you laughed.

"I wish I could tell you that this city was just another myth, but it's not. It smacks too much of reality."

"Well *what else*!" I cried, exasperated with you. First it's a whale house, then you want it to be a myth— couldn't it just be a city, for heaven's sake?"

"Precisely. That's precisely what it is. Let's have coffee."

We walked past the City Hall and I asked you what the little concrete bubble was for.

"Why that's the egg, the seed," you said.

"Of *what*?"

"Why, Lucas George, I'm surprised at you! Of the *whale*, of course! Come on!"

"Looks like a clamshell to me," I said. "Did I ever explain to you where mankind came from, Aaron? A clamshell, half-open, with all the little faces peering out . . . . "

"I'll buy that," you said. "It's a clamshell. Come on!"

I got a job in construction, working on the high beams of a bank that was going up downtown. "Heights don't bother you Indians at all, do they?" the foreman asked me. "No," I said. "We like tall things."

He told me they needed some rivetting work done on the top, and some guys that had gone up couldn't take it—it was too high even for them. So I went up, and the cold steel felt strange against my skin and I sensed long tremors in the giant skeleton of the bank, and it was as though the building was alive, shivering, with bones and sinews and tendons, with a life of its own. I didn't trust it, but I went up and up and there was wind all around me. The city seemed to fall away and the voices of the few men who accompanied me sounded strangely hollow and unreal in the high air. There were four of us—a tosser to heat the rivets and throw them to the catcher who caught them in a tin cup and lowered them with tongs into their holes—a riveter who forced them in with his gun, and a bucker to hold a metal plate on one end of the hole. They told me their names as the elevator took us to the top—Joe, Charlie, Amodeo. I was the bucker.

Amodeo offered me a hand when we first stepped out onto a beam, but I couldn't accept it, although the first minute up there was awful. I watched how Amodeo moved; he was small and agile and treated the beams as though they were solid ground. His smile was swift and confident. I *did* take his hand later, but only to shake it after I had crossed the first beam. I kept telling myself that my people were the People of the Eagle so I of all men should have no fear to walk where the eagles fly. Nevertheless when we ate lunch, the sandwich fell down into my stomach a long long way as though my stomach was still on the ground somewhere, and my throat was the elevator that had carried us up.

I found that holding the metal plate over the rivet holes gave me a kind of support and I was feeling confident and almost happy until the riveter came along and aimed his gun and WHIIRR-TA-TA-TAT, WHIIRR-TA-TA-TAT! My spine was jangling and every notch in it felt like a metal disc vibrating against another metal disc.

After a while, though, I got the knack of applying all sorts of pressure to the plate to counteract some of the vibration. And when the first day was over I was awed to think I was still alive. The next day I imagined that the bank was a huge totem, or the strong man Aemaelk who holds the world up, and I started to like the work.

I didn't see you much those days for I was tired every night, but once I remember we sat over coffee in a restaurant and there was an odd shaky light in your eyes, and you looked sick. A man at a nearby table was gazing out onto the street, dipping a finger from time to time into his coffee and sucking it. I asked you why he was so sad. "He's not a whale," you answered.

"Then what is he?" I asked.

"He's a little salmon all the whales are going to eat," you said. "Like you, like me."

"Where are you working now, Aaron?"

"In a sewer. You go up, Lucas, and I go down. It fits. Right now I'm a mole and you're the eagle."

Aaron, I've got to finish this letter right now. I don't have time to write all I wanted to, because my trial's coming up and I already know how it's going to turn out. I didn't have time to say much about the three years I spent here, about losing the job, about wandering around the city without money, about drinking, about fooling around, about everything falling round me like the totems falling, about getting into that argument in the tavern, and the fat man who called me a dirty Indian, about how I took him outside into a lane and beat him black and blue and seeing his blood coming out and suddenly he was dead. You know it all anyway, there's no point telling it again. Listen, Aaron, what I want to know now is:

Is my grandfather still telling lies to the history-hunters in Skidegate?

Are the moles and the eagles and the whales coming out of the sewers and subways and buildings now it's spring?

Have all the totems on my island fallen, or do some still stand?

Will they stick my head up high on a cedar tree like

33

they did to Gunarh?

Will the Street of Walls fall down one day like the totems?

What did you say I would find in the House of the Whale, Aaron? Aaron? Aaron?

THE HAPPIEST MAN IN THE WORLD

Hugh Garner

It had been a typical Friday afternoon at the office, with no hint of what was to come. When he got the news it came to him without warning, as promotions always did at Cambrian Trust.

He'd finished cleaning up his work, locking all his files away except the Routledge portfolio; that he intended to prepare, over the weekend, for the legal department. He'd placed the file in his Slimline attaché case lying open on his desk, and had glanced at his watch. It was 5:35. As usual he was the last of the estate adjustors still in the office.

He'd pulled on his topcoat when Mr. Wilburt, the department head, tapped on the glass of his corner office and with a beckoning finger had summoned him. He'd nodded, picked up his attaché case and hat, and made his way between the empty desks to T.C.'s office.

Without asking him to sit down the older man had raised his balding grey head and asked, "How old are you now?"

"Thirty-eight, sir."

"And you've been with us how long?"

"Ten years. Seven of them as an adjustor."

"I was an adjustor fifteen years," Wilburt said gruffly. "I may as well tell you that it was a toss-up between you and—well, somebody else. Some of us thought you were still a little young for it, but your work record and the business administration degree you received through extension courses—what's that, night school?" Ed nodded.

"Those things made us decide you were the man." The department manager tilted his chair back and said with a slight smile, "Well, Eddy, I guess you're it."

"I'm it?" he'd asked, keeping the sudden flurry beneath his ribs from showing in his question.

"It was all settled this afternoon up in Stan Parker's office," Wilburt said, welcoming him into the Cambrian management team by calling the president by his first name. "I'm leaving at the end of next week for my place at Vero Beach to spend the winter surf-casting. You'll move in here on Monday morning, but I'll be hovering over your shoulder for a couple of days to fill you in on procedures, and work you into the routine."

"You're leaving us for good?" Ed asked, not letting on that the old man's coming retirement had been office gossip for months.

"Yes. I've reached the mandatory age, and my wife Ellen and I have had this little place down in Florida for years. It's been generally boarded up except for a month every winter, or when the kids and their families have used it. We haven't made up our minds yet whether to sell the house up here and move down there permanently or not."

"I'm sorry to see you go, Mr. Wilburt," he'd said, not quite truthfully. Then had added, "After forty years you deserve it, sir."

The old man had laughed, nodding to himself in agreement. "Call me Tom, Eddy. See you Monday morning, when we'll go up to Stan's office to finalize the deal."

"You bet—Tom. And thanks. Thank you very much."

The old man had bent over the papers on his desk and dismissed him with an off-handed wave.

As Ed Grogan stepped from the elevator into the underground car-park of the tall office building he glanced across at his car. His four-year-old black Pontiac suddenly looked shabby standing there in the almost empty garage, but as he walked toward it he thought happily that now he'd be able to trade up to something bigger. Nothing too ostentatious, of course, for the short suburban street in Greenbriar Hills, but something just a little better. There was no doubt in his mind that Jennifer would have her say about spending his salary increase, but she surely wouldn't object to a new car, or to them joining the Greenbriar golf club. Most of her friends belonged to it, and it would put an end to him having to line up at the tees, with Gord Monroe, at the municipal course in the summer. He remembered the speaker at the Jaycees dinner who had said, "Happiness is success." Tonight Ed Grogan was the happiest man in the world.

He smiled and nodded to the uniformed watchman as he drove out of the garage, and found himself having to curb a joyful urge to hit the gas just a little harder as he turned along the downtown street. Some of them thought him "square," and maybe he was, but the years of hard work, study and attention to detail had paid off after all. He eased his foot on the gas pedal; he couldn't let his euphoria blow everything for him now.

He thought of the others in the office, some of whom would be drinking now in the Paradise Room, as they did every Friday evening. The Paradise Room had been just one of the things he'd had to sacrifice over the years, in order to continue his schooling, to placate Jennifer and to get ahead. He wondered if any of the others from the office had ever realized there'd been times, many times, when he'd envied them. He'd never really learned to drink, or like it, but mixing with the others at the Paradise might have eased his loneliness, and shown them what he was *really* like.

The traffic on the parkway had passed its rush-hour peak, and Ed kept his speed just under five miles above the limit, watching out for both Friday-night drunks and the unmarked police cars that patrolled the road. He stuck to the middle traffic lane, letting those in a hurry pass by on the left, while avoiding the right-hand lane with its slower traffic turning off at the exit ramps.

He tried to keep his exultation in check but his thoughts remained on what this promotion meant to him, and especially to Jennifer. Now she'd be able to have a woman come in one day a week, just like the Bracketts. After all, Carl Brackett was only a sales supervisor for an air-conditioning firm, and according to street gossip the Bracketts were in debt up to their eyeballs.

Greenbriar Hills was only a fifteen-minute run up the parkway, now almost a part of the city to those who lived in the newer subdivisions farther out. Ten years ago, when he'd bought his new home there before the parkway was finished, it had taken him three-quarters of an hour to get downtown. As one of the then-new outer suburbs, it had been called by its developers "The in-place for young families on their way up."

Ten years ago, of course, he hadn't really been on his way anywhere, with his dead-end job in the railroad freight office. Then everything had happened at once. He'd met Jennifer, who was "in social service work," when she was on the rebound from a broken courtship. She'd been aggressively ardent in those days, and they'd been forced into a hasty marriage. His mother had passed away, leaving him just enough money to put a down payment on the house, and furnish it.

It had been Jenny (as she'd let him call her then), through vague connections, who had secured him the interview and the subsequent job at the trust company. It was true, as they said, that behind every successful man was an ambitious wife.

For one exhilarating moment he wondered if his new job would help him convince Jennifer they should have another baby. It wasn't healthy for young Colin to be an only child. Up to now she had countered his hints with the excuse that they couldn't afford another baby just yet. Several of her women friends had only one child too, a token claim to womanhood, but one that least restricted them socially.

He turned off the parkway at the Greenbriar cloverleaf, and at the posted residential speed limit followed the winding streets to his house. The rollaway garage door beneath the window of the master bedroom was open, though he'd complained to Jennifer and ten-year-old Colin to keep it closed so that the smaller children on the street wouldn't take things from his workbench or spill his paint. Since Jennifer's last asthmatic attack over a year ago he had been relegated to the smaller bedroom next to Colin's.

After locking the car in the garage he entered the house through the connecting door and shouted from the kitchen, "Jennifer, I'm home!"

"Your supper's in the oven," came her flat reply from the living-room. "You're late. Colin and I couldn't wait." It was a habit of hers to tack an admonitory ending to almost every answer she gave him, but after ten years he hardly noticed it.

He opened the oven door and took out a lukewarm dish containing the remains of a tuna casserole. Jennifer must have been playing bridge all afternoon, or shopping again with Elsa DeBrough, a friend who was a sort of amateur sculptor and home decorator.

As he took a plate and cup and saucer from a cupboard he thought nostalgically of the family dishes his mother had served: short ribs, beef stews, even shepherd's pie. The teapot was cold, so he filled the kettle and brewed himself a fresh pot of tea. Jennifer and Colin must have had an early supper for things to have grown as cold as they were. The frenetic sounds of a family comedy show came from the TV set in the living room.

After he had eaten, the glow of happiness over his promotion came back to him, and he took a cigar from a half-empty box he had received from the firm last Christmas, and lighted it. Clenching it between his teeth he tried to act out a young-executive fantasy as he washed up the supper things, including the casserole dish. Then he headed for the living-room.

Jennifer, wearing a quilted housecoat, her hair freshly done in an upswept style, reclined on the sofa. Her eyes remained fixed on the television tube and her mouth was set in the half smile she always wore when watching a favourite show. Colin lolled in a chair with his long legs climbing up its back, a bored expression on his face. He didn't look up when his father entered the room.

When a commercial interrupted the program Jennifer looked up and said, "Hi, dear. Have a good day?"

"A great one," he said, exhaling a cloud of cigar smoke as he sat down in an empty chair.

"Dear, I've asked you not to smoke those things in

here," his wife said, curling her lip. "I've had such a day, traipsing all over town with Elsa."

"Your new hairdo looks fine, though I think I like it better when you wear it long."

"Oh, Edward ... " she said, with an exasperated little laugh.

"How've you been, Colin?" he asked.

"All right," the boy answered, without looking up.

"Sssh!" she cautioned as the program returned to the screen.

After a brief glance at the show he looked over at his wife. For some reason she reminded him of the asexual slim thirtyish models who advertised nail polish, profile pointed away from the camera, her manicured fingers displayed in her lap. Jennifer's looks *were* those of a modish middle-class executive's wife, he thought happily. When they occasionally attended functions together he was proud to introduce her, stretching himself as tall as he could to equal their heights.

He took his cigar into the hallway, and picked up his mail from the antique table the DeBrough woman had palmed off on them. He shuffled it through his hands: the electric bill, an announcement from Rotary, a charitable request from his church, the monthly statement from Group Investors Inc., a letter bearing the postmark of the town where his sister Norma lived, and a mauve envelope that Jennifer must have opened by mistake. He took a typewritten mauve sheet from the opened envelope and glanced at the signature. Karen Grierson. He read the note, a request for a job recommendation. Now he remembered who Karen Grierson was, a young typist who had taken the place of Mrs. Cluff, down at the office, the summer before.

He smiled warmly to himself at the memory of the girl. She'd been a crazily alive little thing who said things like, "I dig," and, "Shall I stash this in the files, Mr. Grogan?" He carried the letter into the kitchen and put it in an inside pocket of his suit coat. He was touched that she'd requested a recommendation from *him*.

Carrying the rest of the letters in his hand he returned to the living-room just as Jennifer's comedy show came to an end.

"Your friends the Bracketts are moving," his wife said. They'd been "your friends" to her since the Sunday afternoon he'd crossed the street to give Carl Brackett a hand with a small auto-repair job. He'd stayed and had a couple of cold beers with Carl and his wife in their kitchen.

"They're moving! Where to?"

"A downtown apartment, I hear. I guess their debts have finally caught up with them."

He glanced quickly at young Colin. "I don't think it's that, Jennifer."

"*You* can stick up for them if you like." She wafted some imaginary cigar smoke away from her face. Colin uncoiled himself from the chair and left the room.

Ed said, "It finally happened, Jennifer. I'm taking over Wilburt's desk on Monday."

She sat up straight and smiled. "So he's retiring? It's about time." She crossed the floor and placed her arms dutifully around his neck. "I'm pleased, Edward. I'm glad you beat out Thompson and that icky old Peterson."

He circled her with his arm. Until then he hadn't thought of the promotion as being a contest between himself and the other adjustors, but now he suddenly realized that Peterson and Thompson both had more seniority than he. The realization appalled him.

Being careful of her hairdo she brushed his cheek with her lips, but when he pushed himself to his feet and tried to kiss her she drew herself away with a practised twist. "Not now, dear ... Colin's here ... ," she whispered. She left the room, smiling over her shoulder. He sat down again and opened his sister's letter.

It was the usual summary of the month's events relating to herself, her druggist husband and her two pretty daughters. As he read her misspelled scrawl he felt a warm family feeling creep over him, and he made up his mind to visit them around Christmas, whether Jennifer came or not.

He carried the rest of the mail into his den, where he wrote out a couple of cheques and filed the investment statement. He caught a whiff of Jennifer's expensive

41

perfume on himself, and smiled at the promise implied in her words, "Not now, dear . . . . "

A little later Jennifer came to the door and said, "Edward, I think we should have a few friends drop in tomorrow evening to celebrate, don't you?"

"Yes. That'll be fine, dear."

"It won't be a regular party or anything like that. Just the DeBroughs, Hamiltons, Sylvia and Merv Appel, and the new member of the bridge club, Bette Parks, and her husband."

"How about Gord and Edna Monroe? After all we owe them an invite after them taking us to the club dance in September."

"Not this time, dear. You know how Gordon Monroe drinks."

She had a legitimate point there. "All right, I'll leave it to you," he said.

"And, Edward, I'm out of cigarettes. Would you drive over to the plaza and pick me up a pack?"

"While I'm there I may as well get a couple of bottles of Scotch too," he said.

"Don't forget Elsa drinks nothing but gin."

"We have gin."

"Colin wants to go to one of the stores in the plaza too. While you're gone I'll phone everybody."

Driving over to the shopping plaza Ed tried to draw his son out on the subject of his school work, but the boy answered him in monosyllables. When he parked in an empty parking space in front of the liquor store Colin jumped out, saying he was going to pick up some tubes of paint at the hobby shop. Ed was proud of his son's ability as a painter; even his schoolteacher had written Jennifer praising the boy's work.

He ran into Carl and Grace Brackett outside the liquor store, and they exchanged pleasantries on the sidewalk. They didn't mention their moving, so he didn't bring it up. Both invited him over to their house later for a drink, but he excused himself. "I'm getting some Scotch for tomorrow night," he told them. "Jennifer is having some of her friends drop in."

"That'll be nice," Grace said.

42

Carl Brackett pretended to let his bag of liquor slip from his hands, and Grace berated him. "Brackett, you drop that and it's the divorce court for you!" They all laughed.

Ed watched the Bracketts heading for the supermarket, both wearing old sweaters and slacks, bumping each other with their hips as they walked, and laughing. He envied them the fun they seemed to get out of living.

When he came out of the liquor store he helped a shabby man open his car door, and watched smiling as four or five children piled into the old second-hand car, their harassed father struggling with two big bags of groceries. It reminded him of the gypsy-like families he and Jennifer had passed on the highways on their trip once to Yellowstone; second-hand station wagons and old pick-up trucks piled with camping paraphernalia and kids. For just a fleeting moment he felt he had lost something from life.

When the man with the children vacated the parking space next to his, Ed sat in his car waiting for Colin to return from the hobby shop. A white convertible with the top up, and two men in the front seat, pulled past the empty space, then began backing into it. Ed saw that they weren't going to make it, and he blew a warning on his horn. The driver ignored it, and there was a rather heavy bump on one front corner of his car, followed by a scraping sound. The convertible completed its reversing into the space, and straightened out about a foot away from Ed's car. He had to slide across the front seat to get out through the right-hand door.

He walked to the front of his car, and looked down to see what damage had been done. It seemed that only his front bumper had been bent slightly out of line. The convertible, however, had a long indentation along its front fender and door. Both its occupants climbed out of the driver's side and came around to where Ed was standing.

"You don't seem to have done any damage to me," Ed said. "I blew my horn to warn you that you were turning too tight."

The men ignored him, and stood staring at the long

ugly scar that ran along the convertible's white-painted side. One of them, a pot-bellied man wearing a purple-and-yellow hockey club windbreaker, its sleeves and front decorated with adolescent crests and badges, said, "you'll pay for this, mister."

"What!"

"You heard me," the man said. Ed noticed that he was about his own age but a little taller. "Look where you're parked," the man snarled, "nearly over the white dividing line an' at least a foot too far forward."

Ed looked. His car *was* up against the white line, but not across it. He'd been forced to crowd over to the left by a big car parked on the other side of him, that had now gone. "I'm still parked on my side of the line," he said quietly.

"A smart guy eh? One a these Greenbriar Hills punks thinks he owns everything around here, eh?"

Ed noticed now that the man was drunk, waving on his feet as he shoved his face forward belligerently. A small group of shoppers, arms loaded with paper bags, began to gather in a wide semi-circle around them. Some teenagers drifted over from where they'd been lounging in front of a hamburger bar. "Give 'im a rap on the mouth!" a thin, string-haired girl screamed shrilly. Her companions began to goad the drunk.

The man in the windbreaker looked around, saw the crowd, and said, " 'at's what I should do, give 'im a rap in the mouth." He turned to his companion, a tall sober-looking man wearing a dress shirt and tie covered by a cardigan. "Waddya think, Walt?"

"Take it easy, Johnny," his friend said.

The drunk turned to Ed. "Walt here's a lawyer, an' he'll tell ya we can sue. Take this guy's licence, Walt, an' see if he's got insur'nce."

The reference to insurance angered Ed more than anything else. Did this drunken lout think he would drive without being fully covered against accidents? "We'll get a policeman," he said. "I don't show my licence to anyone else."

"Fuzz lover!" screeched the teenage virago, while her companions heckled him.

"Waddya mean, cop?" the drunk asked, breaking from his friend's grasp and reaching for Ed's lapels. Ed backed away, bringing derisive jeers from the young punks. The drunk, encouraged by the falsetto shouts of his long-haired claque, gave Ed a short jab to the nose, jolting him back against his car.

The unexpected blow surprised Ed, but he was more surprised to find that his nose was bleeding, a rivulet of blood running down across his lips. Through his watering eyes he saw the pot-bellied man drawing his fist back to hit him again, and in a mixture of fear and rage he raised his arms and stumbled forward, swinging wildly. One of his fists connected with something sharp, and when he stumbled on something and opened his eyes he looked down and saw the drunk pushing himself to his knees and shaking his head. The man's bridgework jutted horribly from between his lips.

The man's tall friend helped him to his feet, and hustled him away through the crowd, as the teenagers quickly switched their partisanship to the winner, and began a raucous mocking chant as they followed the two departing men. The crowd now broke up, the noise it was making coming from a long distance in pulsating waves. Ed took a handkerchief from his pocket and pressed it over his nose and mouth, holding on to the hood of the car as his legs began to tremble. He got into the car again, and pushed himself along the seat to the driver's side.

Now that it was over he felt a strange mixture of disgust and elation, something he couldn't remember ever having felt before. He dabbed at his nose until the bleeding stopped. When he looked down he noticed that the blood had run off his chin on to his shirt and tie, and there were a few spots on the lapels of his suit.

He hadn't noticed Colin getting into the car, but the boy was sitting beside him now, a fancy paper bag clutched on his knees. Ed hurriedly shoved his bloodied handkerchief into his pocket, and keeping his face averted asked the boy, "Are those your paints?"

"Yes."

"Good."

With the nervous care of a learning driver he slowly eased the car out of its parking space, joined a short line of cars at the exit from the parking lot, and when his turn came swung carefully into the street and drove toward home.

"Who was the man you beat up, Dad?" Colin asked him.

"I don't know. A silly man who scraped the side of his car when he was backing in next to me."

"A kid told me he used to be a hockey player. I guess they're not so tough, eh?"

"Oh, hockey players are pretty tough; they have to be. It's a rough sport. Maybe he wasn't much of a hockey player."

"*You* knocked him down."

"I was just lucky, I guess. Two grown men fighting like that is crazy."

"You broke his false teeth, Dad. You gave him three or four good ones before he even knew what happened."

"Did I? It was because I was scared I guess."

"You weren't scared. You must have been tough before you—when you were young, eh?"

"No, Skip," he said, giving the boy back a nickname that his wife had discouraged years before. "That was the first time I hit anyone since leaving school." He ruffled Colin's hair. "It's better not to fight."

"Not all the time," the boy said.

He smiled down at his son, and caught the boy's admiring glance, for the first time that he remembered.

As soon as he pulled into the garage Colin ran into the house. Ed locked the garage door, and followed the boy, the package of liquor held in his arm. Jennifer was waiting for him in the kitchen, and he knew from her expression that Colin had already told her about the fight. She said nothing, her eyes flashing with a cold loathing.

He stared critically at his face in a small kitchen mirror. His nose was slightly swollen, and there was dried blood on his mouth and chin and where he had wiped it across one of his cheeks. His shirt collar and necktie were a mess. He placed the liquor on the table, and walked to the short flight of back stairs leading to the upper level of the house and the bathroom.

"How could you!" Jennifer spat out. "How could you make a public spectacle of yourself right up here in the Greenbriar Plaza?"

He turned and stared at her wearily.

"In front of your own son, and—and—God knows who else!"

He stared at her as if seeing her for the first time.

"You could have been arrested! Tonight of all nights!" She whimpered in self-sympathy. "I've already called the Parks, the Appels and Hamiltons, and Elsa—"

He turned away from her, cutting off her whimpering words with the total unexpectedness of his action. As he stepped on the first stair she screamed, "Where's my cigarettes?"

He faced her again and said quietly, "I'm sorry; I forgot them." Then he took the car keys from his pocket and laid them on the sink counter. "You'll have to get them yourself," he said.

She stared at the keys, then took a couple of steps toward the stairs and shouted triumphantly, "Some drunken woman called you on the phone. She sounded as if she was in a bar."

He shrugged and made his way upstairs.

In the bathroom he took off his jacket, shirt and tie, and washed the dried blood from his face and neck. Then he bent over the wash-basin and laved his nose with cold water. It felt tender beneath his fingers, but it wasn't broken.

Carrying the clothes he had removed, he went along the hallway to his own room. As he passed Colin's open door he glanced in at his son, who was sitting on the edge of his bed with his new tubes of paint in his hand. The boy looked up at him with a shy smile, and Ed said, "Take it easy, Skip," and winked.

In his room he took everything from the pockets of his suit, and laid the items on the dresser, throwing the suit into a corner along with his soiled shirt and tie. He pulled on a faded blue sweatshirt, threaded his belt

47

through the loops of a pair of slacks, and pulled them on. He methodically placed the items he had taken from his suit pants into the pockets of his slacks, picking up young Karen Grierson's letter and smiling at it before transferring it to a rear pocket. After combing his hair he went downstairs to the living room, and threw himself into a chair.

The ringing of the telephone startled him, and he heard Jennifer answer it on the kitchen extension. "It's for you!" she shouted.

Picking up the hall phone he said, "Hello. Ed Grogan here." He knew Jennifer was listening in the kitchen.

A shrill drunken woman's voice croaked, "Congratulations, Grogan, you little louse." From behind the voice he could hear conversation, the clink of glasses, and the sound of a musical combo. "What's a matter, Grogan, you got nothing to say?"

The voice was too young to belong to either Mrs. Peterson or Mrs. Thompson, even if they had been the kind of women who would call him like that.

More shrilly now, the voice said, "The whole estate department's against you, Grogan, even old man Wilburt! Don't think you're—"

"Whose wife or mistress are you?" Ed asked gently. When there was no answer he asked, "Where are you, down at the Paradise Room?"

There was a hurried click at the end of the line, followed by that of the kitchen extension. He remained sitting at the telephone table, marvelling sadly at the universal meanness shared by all the frightened, frustrated people in the world. In a moment he heard the garage door being rolled up, and the sound of his car being backed down the driveway.

He pulled young Karen's folded mauve letter from his back pocket and read it again, letting the young girl's friendliness drive the hurt and sadness from his mind. When he returned it to his pocket, the sadness remained, but it was eased now by the knowledge that his son had learned to respect him, if for reasons he had never dreamed of until that night.

He had acted tough toward the guy in the plaza out

of fright, and to the harpy on the telephone out of anger, but neither of these incidents were indicative of change. Things had gone on too long as they had been to be changed. To become something he wasn't, now, would need a complete change of personality. He might be a square, and his values might be wrong to some people, but these were things that had become part of him over his thirty-eight years, and it was too late to change them now. Even if he wished to. He sighed.

When the phone rang again he stepped into the hall and jerked the receiver from its cradle, shouting, "Hello!"

A man's laughing voice said, "Take it easy, killer. It's Carl."

"Carl Brackett?" Ed laughed with relief. "I'm sorry, Carl, I was expecting a different kind of call."

"Grace and I saw you flatten that professional Frank Merriwell in the plaza. It's about time somebody took that Little League jerk outa the playoffs."

"It was a fluke, Carl. Believe me, I didn't want—"

"Just a minute, Grace wants to talk to you."

"Hi, Ed. Listen, if you need a couple of witnesses or anything, Carl and I saw the whole thing. I decided old butterfingers here should put the bottled goods in the car before we went over to the supermarket, so that's how we saw what happened. How about you and your wife dropping over for a drinky-poo, as the crazy broad next door to us always calls it?"

"Thanks. Jennifer's gone over for some cigarettes, but I'll ask her when she comes back. I hear you two are moving off the street?"

"Boy, how the news gets around up here! Yeah we are, Ed. Now that young Alice is married and Libby's gone to nursing school we figured we'd fob off this Bauhaus Gothic on to some social upward achiever, as the psychologists call them. We're moving to a downtown apartment to ride the subway." There was the sound of a short scuffle. When Grace returned to the line she said, "I just stole Carl's drink; he was already one up on me. Come on over if you can, Ed. We'd love to have you."

Ed hung up the phone and went back to the living-room. Though the Bracketts were ten years older than he and

49

Jennifer were, they seemed ten years younger than he and his wife had ever been. He hated to see them move away.

When he heard Jennifer bring the car back, he walked into the kitchen and passed on the Brackett's invitation.

"I don't feel up to your friends tonight," she snapped. "I'm going up to my bed."

The way she emphasized "my bed" showed him how much things had changed since he'd left home for the shopping plaza a short time before. He watched her slim legs cross the kitchen and disappear up the back stairs.

"The happiest man in the world," he said, now mocking the way he'd said it earlier in the evening. Then he laughed a bitter joyless laugh. Taking one of the bottles of Scotch from the bag on the table, and without following his usual routine of shutting the garage door or putting out the lights, he went through the house to the front door, opened it, and slammed it noisily behind him. With the bottle swinging in his hand he headed across the street to where the beckoning lights, and life and love, shone through the Bracketts' picture window.

AGATHE

Nora Keeling

He smiles and imagines that I am smiling at him in return. Then my rocking-chair creaks a bit and I smile more widely. My smile is dusty, he said once, like my being. But my teeth are the only part of me not wholly my own, so he oughtn't to compare dustinesses. He calls me Agathe, which is correct, but he pronounces it as though it could be pronounced in English. He always has. For forty years he has pronounced it in such a manner. Now it matters less.

Today he brought me a box of chocolates. I never eat them. I laughed and laughed. He imagined that I laughed with pleasure. I rarely inform him of his errors anymore. In fact, I laughed at the avarice of this sixty-year carcase of a man. I laughed more when I perceived that he thought I laughed out of gratefulness. He ought to know after having been legally married to me for forty years that a box of candy with ribbons on it will never make me forget . . . .

In leaving he said goodbye. He always does. Every week after his visit he says goodbye. Then he stoops to kiss me on the forehead, as though there were any affection between us. But I busy myself with anything I can find, to deter him from touching me. I say goodbye in my turn and lead him to the door. Then I lock the door, fastening all three locks with care.

One week, perhaps it was in a month of September, I didn't answer the door. He fretted. He telephoned later. Then he finally sent the maid to see if I was all right.

She assured him that I had merely been sleeping when he came. I confirmed the tale later. In fact I had been wide awake. I stood not far from the door. Later I regretted my act. For I was deprived of the joy of sitting and smiling at him all during his visit, and of thinking all the while where the best place to shoot him would be. Would the belly be best, or the genitals or the head? The problem preoccupies me. If I were a good shot, I should perhaps not be tormented by such a question.

My son John tries to dissuade me from my purpose. I call him Pious because of his attitude. He dislikes the nickname intensely. Bùt I take delight in annoying him. I didn't used to. He was once a good son and obedient. Now he's ungrateful. All sons are, they say. But a son who refuses to help me rid my rooms of the carcase of my husband, after I have shot him, is certainly a useless appendage. I told him this. He smiled the way I do when I torment people. He smiled because he doesn't even believe that I have a revolver. I have had one for thirty years. It sits under a young girl's nightdress that I have never worn, that was bought for me, in the bottom drawer of my oak dresser. It makes me smile to think of it.

He doesn't believe I have the weapon, the greatest joy of my life. He doesn't believe that I have my justification. In any case, he thinks I am mad—harmlessly so. I flatter the belief. I speak of butterflies in the wintertime and of starving sparrows in the summer. I say that they too are in my drawer. He never checks for himself. I speak of ribbons hanging from the ears of my spaniel, and of pearls hanging from the end of the tail of the Burmese cat, Lucifer. And then I smile a little more, while Pious wonders embarrassedly what to do with his great limbs that flop and hang like those of a scarecrow. His water-blue eyes avoid mine, insipid eyes, those of a coward—like his father. He fingers things with long bony fingers—fingers like those of his father, hanging from the end of bony, white hands whose blue veins stick through like so many lines in a geography book. But Pious was never fat as his father is—a fatness acquired in part from drinking too much Pernod and too much beer during the year we spent together touring Holland and Germany and France and Spain. He pretended then that we were happy newlyweds. He pretended it when others were around. He never dared pretend with me. He didn't dare pretend even when he was about the conceiving of our ungrateful son. He simply grunted and pushed mechanically as men do. I asked him afterward if he felt better and he said no. I replied that it was a pity, in that case, that he had subjected me to such a rude and undignified type of torture. I saw to it that he never did so again. I did what people in novels do and I ran away. But he wouldn't even consent to a legal separation.

Then I ejected Pious into the world—at that time he was John. For many years I imagined that one day he might help me. I raised him in such a hope. I failed as I have done in almost all of the enterprises that I have taken up. But I will not fail in the most important task that I have to do. If I haven't accomplished it successfully already, it is only because the thought of doing so is my greatest pleasure. If only the realization of the act is as sweet as the thought of it. But afterward—what will I have to live for?

There is no doubt that I will outlive my act.

I could perhaps continue writing in order that the whole tale might be laid bare. In this way I may relive the sweetest moments, and most particularly the moment of success. Surely if I can live it vividly before the fact, I will find it a double pleasure after the act.

Tomorrow the fleshy wretch will visit me again.

Each night before he comes I ask myself with a shudder if tomorrow I shall finally arrive at completion. The drawer is so inviting. The image of how his face will contort as I take the weapon out of its nest is sweeter than the moment of motherhood. It isn't surprising that I have hesitated for so long. In dying he may take my best moments with him.

But it is time for bed. I would do well to be refreshed and rested for the visit. It is so much easier to torment him with words when my mind is alert. I can remember at just what point to remind him of his pale and hanging flesh. Sixty years surround him like a prison.

How slowly the time between visits drags.

Tom-Tom made his visit. What delightful moments I spent. Immediately upon his arrival he set the television going. He made me a gift of the thing when I was only fifty. I never watch the television. But sometimes I let him watch it, so that I may observe the expression on his face when pretty young women appear on the screen.

His agitation gives me more pleasure than anyone might imagine. Today I was not in the humour. After he had settled himself in the chair that is reserved especially for him, lowering his flabby buttocks onto the large pillowed seat in a movement that reminds me of garbage settling onto the ground on a hot June day, he adjusted the picture box until a group of dancing girls appeared. I bore the spectacle for a few minutes, then inquired of him what possible pleasure he could derive from the sight of so many human females shaking their faeces and their liquid refuse about. He shut the box off. But the comment aroused visions in me of his own tripe and I was obliged to force myself to think of other things. I took the box of chocolates he had offered me during his last visit and began distributing them one by one to Thisby, the spaniel. Tom-Tom's face contorted, but he said nothing, so I offered the ribbon to Lucifer. The effect was still unsatisfactory. Then I asked about Pious, whom Tom-Tom had no doubt seen more recently than I. The good doctor often asked me how it could be that I had so little affection for my own son. I replied that the question preoccupied me little, but that I didn't exactly dislike him, except when I considered his source, the slimy result of Tom-Tom's libido; whenever I dwelt on such a thought, Pious did indeed fill me with repugnance.

—How do I know he is mine?

—Nobody else could produce such a milk-sop.

The answer seemed to satisfy him. At least it cured him of pursuing the problem of Pious' paternity. Then I inquired about his secretary, Sulvana. The inquiry always troubled him. The girl, in exchange for some small gratifications from the doctor, gratified him. She had been doing so for two years now. I wondered aloud what bed they used, or did they use the couch in the living-room? Did Tom-Tom turn the light out, or did he expose his ungrateful, falling flesh to the girl? Did he ever manage to satisfy her or did he operate like a mechanical sewing-machine, as he did forty years ago? My spouse refused to answer, and assumed his face of paralyzed horror. The expression hasn't amused me for some time now. So I rang for Clemmy, whom Tom-Tom calls my "companion" but who is neither more nor less than a competent maid. I rarely call her to my own room. She too wiggles her lower parts when she walks. I dislike people who juggle their intestines around as though to remind one of the least appetizing part of their humanity. Moreover, the girl giggles. But Tom-Tom likes her, and he drops all his masks when female flesh and blood goes through its contortions to please him. I wondered, again aloud, whether he had ever managed to have this one. He blushed and ran his fingers through his sticky hair, amazed that I could talk thus in the presence of the girl. But Clemmy seldom listens, and even if she had . . . .

I asked for tea for the good doctor. Tea was part of our ritual. I knew he would have preferred a beer or a whisky, depending on the weather. He gulped the hot brew down nonetheless while I observed him, adjusting my spectacles as I did so.

I rarely drink or eat things prepared by other people. I am not afraid of being poisoned. But I doubt the competence of others. It doesn't equal my own.

By now, Thisby was burping and smelling up the room, perhaps because of the chocolates he had swallowed. Tom-Tom didn't seem to notice, so I had the girl remove the dog until his slight upset was past. He left, disconcerted by his own functionings.

Lucifer, who like all cats has no gift of discrimination, was climbing onto the doctor's shoulders and sniffing round his hair. I made a mental note to have the cat washed with a new dry product that has been advertised lately, and allowed him to continue. Tom-Tom dislikes cats.

Then, tired of the effort, I began to yawn. It was my

habitual procedure when I had had enough nonsense. Tom-Tom hoisted his hulking carcase into a standing position. He took his leave of me in his habitual fashion. I replied in mine. I remarked too that his frame had left its usual mark on the upholstery of the great chair. Two sunken areas indicated where he had deposited his rump. Averting my gaze, I called for the girl to come and remove the chair. She dragged it to its domicile: a large, dark closet I never use, which houses the chair and any of the doctor's effects he may have forgotten. Tom-Tom knew about this. Like Pious, he pretended to attribute it to harmless madness, or to senility. The girl didn't seem to mind what others termed my eccentricities. She was too dull to have guessed their meaning. In any case, she had a job that suited her. I seldom interfered with her management of things. I rarely called her. And I cared little about how she conducted her private life.

As she left, I looked at the drawer that held the weapon. It sat there unobtrusively. The nightdress closed around it like a vulva. Such a thought made me bang the drawer shut.

I reflected upon the stupidity of people who believe that murders only happen in books. I considered their deterministic use of the verb "happen." Things don't always just happen.

Today when the sad piece of flesh came to visit, I terminated the whole session quickly by asking him why he couldn't simply die and spare me the commission of a crime. He laughed. I was impervious to him. He left, stopping in the kitchen to indulge in a game of hide and seek with the girl. He must have managed to corner her in short order, for I heard timid giggles rising and falling at intervals. In case he had actually caught her, I didn't go to the kitchen to interrupt their intimacy. I dreaded being exposed to any part of him in a state of undress. Most particularly, I knew that I shouldn't rapidly recover from the spectacle of that elongated chunk of meat that filled him so with pride, as it sat up in supplication. Or did it still? Yes, certainly it must. Otherwise the television box wouldn't affect him as it did, nor would Clemmy.

I pushed all such reflections from my mind by resuming my reading of Pascal's autobiography. I liked the man for having decided to submit to a paralysis of his lower limbs.

I was occupied with remorse for a crime that I hadn't yet committed. The sentiment wasn't new. The thought that this poor wretch should die when he was still capable of enjoying existence in his own animal fashion seemed to me unjust, despite his sins.

Thus occupied, I was surprised when he entered. I had almost forgotten that this was his day—as he called it. The sight of him wiped away all remorse. We passed our hour as we usually do. He drank his tea as he always does. The girl had added cookies to the collation. I idly distributed some to Thisby. Shortly after the refreshments, the dog began again to befoul the air of the room. I had him taken by the girl, who did so with the habitual waggling of her posterior. Tom-Tom's hypnotized gaze after her buttocks annoyed me more than usual. I asked aloud if perhaps I were not being slightly unfair in sending the dog from the room. There was nothing to prove that it wasn't the good doctor himself who was emitting such bad odours. Indeed, not only were foul smells consistent with his character; it would also be like him to break wind as stealthily as he did everything else.

At first Tom-Tom merely regarded me with rage. But he was accustomed to what he called my insults, which I knew to be factual statements—and he contented himself with asking me why I dwelt so frequently on subjects having to do with the viscera. I replied that the weekly spectacle of a breathing dung-hill made my pre-occupation understandable enough. He would have left puffing and swearing under his breath, if the girl hadn't reappeared to take away the dishes. She puttered about long enough to make him forget his wound. I asked that Thisby be re-admitted.

The drawer gaped open. Tom-Tom was also accustomed to that. He had once asked me why I, such an overly-neat person, should be so negligent with this one drawer. I replied that it was broken, that nonetheless the dresser

57

had been my grandmother's, and that I would exchange it for no other, nor would I have a clumsy carpenter mess about with it. This seemed to Tom-Tom to fit in with my fanaticism about certain pieces of my personal property. So I could leave it slightly ajar at all times, during his presence. Thus I could rarely forget what I had set out to do.

Either Thisby had relieved himself or the good doctor was practising continence, for the air remained clearer than usual. I remarked upon this in a dry voice. It was enough to make Tom-Tom hoist his frame to a vertical position and take his leave. This time he didn't make a movement to kiss me goodbye. I thanked him audibly for his understanding in not doing so. The girl then came in to cart the chair away. I was obliged to recall her afterwards to have her put the rug to rights. A corner had been turned back on itself as she moved the chair.

Then I myself rearranged the knick-knacks that Tom-Tom had been toying with. He is a nervous wretch. The knick-knack shelf was put next to his chair precisely so that he might have something to play with as he talked or listened or ogled the girl. I shouldn't like him to handle things that I was fond of. I next washed my hands. After all this I was free to meditate about how Racine must have felt after poisoning his mistress. For I was of the same opinion as some of the poet's critics. That is, I found him guilty. But murder is much commoner than one might think. Moreover, many get away with it.

Only the emotionally immature will find it improbable that a man should sit once a week for an hour or two to hear himself insulted. Remorse looks for its cure. Tom-Tom feels guiltier about his past behaviour than he will admit even to himself. Certain religious people flagellate themselves. Men like the doctor come and look at their crime. Maybe they hope to see it lessen before their eyes. Naturally this man would simply say, if questioned, that he came out of duty. One cannot leave one's old wife to rot alone.

Tom-Tom is gifted with enough self-deception to last him, should he live that long, for 300 years. It is also perhaps to hear a frank opinion of himself that he visits me. I am given a role he cannot play. The truth coming from himself would be too hard to bear. Thus he has two blessings: he can hear the truth; we all must, but he can reject it as he pleases, arguing to himself as he does so that it comes from someone else and that one individual can never be known to another. Perhaps . . . but not so much as certain modern authors would have us believe.

If the world were filled with Tom-Toms, murder would be as frequent as a sneeze.

To make Tom-Tom more uncomfortable on his last visit, I decided to speak once more of old and rusted adventures. At sixty such talk still disturbed him. He couldn't bear others having had what he had been denied. So I launched into one of the episodes best suited to irritate his pride.

—I have always wondered how much cattle can take in.

—Why so?

—Once when I was young and still able to attract young men and be attracted by them, I copulated with one of my favourites on a roadside. It was night-fall. A pasture was in front of us. When I had all but finished, I looked up to see a row of cattle lined up along the fence, staring at us. The spectacle amused me so much that I was unable to finish mating.

Tom-Tom's face became extravagantly ugly. He was angrier than I have seen him in years. But then so also was I. His possessiveness was a trait that I despised. He rose and lumbered from the room, his face as crimson as that part of him that repelled me most of all.

I waited a decent interval. I waited until I heard Clemmy giggle. Then she tittered. Trembling slightly, I retrieved the weapon from its hole. I waited some more. There was a silence in the other room and I thought my heart would burst. Perhaps he had quietly left and I should have to wait for a full week longer. But the girl tittered again, a shriller sound this time, and when the solitary laughter reached a climax of sorts, I opened the door. Astonished, they both stared at me. My weapon was pointed at the proper spot below his grotesque belly. It exploded for what seemed to be a long time.

STILL LIFE COMPOSITION: WOMAN'S CLOTHES

Kent Thompson

Stretching before the mirror over the bathroom sink she was lovely. It was lovely. She smiled into the mirror and didn't see her smile. Only teeth. Recently cleaned by the dentist. He was heavy, clean, efficient. He used mouthwash between patients. White teeth. One two three four five.

The thin white nightgown she threw off was Seeg's favourite. Nude, she bent to brush her teeth. The nipples of her plump breasts touched the cold porcelain of the washbasin, and she giggled—still brushing her teeth.

—Happy as a schoolgirl, she thought. She rinsed her mouth and spat the foamy toothpaste water into the basin. Hadn't she been frightened and proud when her breasts had ripened. A-B-C cup. She sang a scale in her head. Her eyes caught her eyes in the mirror and she growled and roared, spat and rinsed again, in imitation of her husband Seeg when *he* brushed *his* teeth. Argh. Splat. It was lovely. She performed Seeg's glum and serious expression. His vulgarity rising. What knockers!

It was lovely.

She peered out at the spring morning through a slight parting in the curtains. The morning light was a peculiar damp green. As in England or Wales, she thought. Now New Brunswick. The town outside, tucked beneath the trees. Everything was damp and heavy with green. There's a little yellow lost in it somewhere. In the neatly-groomed clearing behind Burnby's Cape Cod house the light was falling through the trees, dappled and yellow. Buttercups beneath the hedge. The yellow lost is found again.

She listened for Seeg. Was he angry this morning? Would he feel the world was chasing him down, boxing him in, wearing him down? At the end of an evening sometimes, when they sat over coffee, they would talk over the endless novel that was the history of his family and hers. If he was in a good mood he would conclude by mocking himself, saying that he was one of the few people in the world who actually got angry at the thought of his own mortality. "I don't want to die," he admitted. "And I'm afraid I'll get so afraid of death that I won't be able to move."

It was true. Sometimes he was so afraid of getting killed in an automobile accident that he had to force himself to leave the sanctuary of the apartment and get in the car and drive it someplace. Anyplace. After all their travels (which Seeg considered dangerous) he was pleased to live in Fredericton, New Brunswick, "because mortality seems slower here."

She liked it because she could taste every bit of life here. She scratched under her breasts with both hands at once.

Seeg said that courage was required to stay alive and avoid a living death. "So I get in the car and I drive it, and I'm all right once I'm in the driver's seat because I'm a good driver (he was), and you have to do these little maniac acts of courage if you want to stay alive."

She listened again for Seeg, and heard the bed creak as he sat up. He would be looking at himself now, sitting on the edge of the bed (and breaking down the springs), looking sombrely at his hairy naked body.

He must be happy this morning, she concluded. She began to sing softly so he would know she was happy. Without thinking, she had begun to sing a song he particularly disliked.

Seeg's voice was saying: "That's the most stupid song in the world. The melody of vomit."

She laughed. "It got you up, didn't it?" And she changed to *The Butcher Boy*, which he liked. "A maid again, I'll never be," she sang, teasing him. "What do you want for breakfast?"

"Cereal."

If he were really angry he would mutter the word, holding back the sarcastic thought that he wouldn't put her to the bother of preparing him a proper breakfast.

"Honest," he said. "Why don't you ever believe that I mean what I say?"

She smiled and kissed him lightly. It was too lovely— too lovely to spend the morning preparing bacon and eggs, which she did for him when he awoke hollow-eyed with the anguish of mortality and economics.

She went back to the bathroom to brush her hair and looked at herself smugly in the mirror. She was a good-looking woman, and she was better to him than she would be if she loved him—because, if she loved him, she would be too much his, and he hers, for these manoeuvrings around the awkwardnesses of domestic life.

It was a lovely morning and in her mirror she was face to face with a face that said she didn't love her husband. My lord, she thought impatiently, my period is due. She found her eyes were filling with tears, and she scratched her muff in derision, to bring back the old mood.

She shook her head to break the name that appeared there.

"Are you up, Seeg?"

"Yes. Lovely morning."

Odd the thing about names. How many wives habitually addressed their husbands by their last names? Jonathan Seeg was always Seeg. Sometimes he would mock himself: "Seeg, Seeg, fat as a pig." But he wasn't fat, although he *did* have the start of the ancestral Seeg pot-belly. "My father had it; I will have it." One more aspect of the eternal cycle which he admitted and admitted disliking.

Seeg. What kind of a name is that? An immigrant name. A North American name. A shortened name. Seigrist? Jewish? No. Just German. Seegmuller. "My grandfather shortened it." She supposed it cost more to paint a sign "Seegmuller's Dry Goods" than it did to print "Seeg's Clothing." The sign swung from the porch of the old house turned into a store on the weak end of Main Street.

While Seeg was in the bathroom she dressed and caught a glimpse of her bare backside in the mirror while she was struggling with her bra. She remembered wondering what X would think of her nude before he had seen her, and — what would he think of her now?

Names. X had a name. (She refused to think of it, however.) At the Kensington party of that LSE chap they had found themselves turned into one another's arms in the kitchen with the terrible old gas cooker. X had been saying, "Hello, what a terrible sink. Looks like hundreds of fat old women have been cut up in it," and as she was turning away from that sink, spilling the water in her whisky glass, she had found herself wrapped into his kiss and pressing into him. When they broke apart X was blinking because she had gone at him with tongue, teeth and claws. "Now," he said, "how did *that* happen?"

"I don't know," she said with embarrassment. "I'm not the sort—usually."

"I know," he said.

"How?"

"I know the sort," he said.

"Oh. Well, I suppose we should introduce ourselves."

But X wouldn't allow this. Don't let's get complicated, he had said. And he wouldn't even let her tell him her name. "Make one up," he insisted.

"Daphne," she said, giggling.

"Right," he said. "Daphne, love, shall we be going off to mummy's place in the country to ride to hounds? Or shall we nip over to daddy's flat and be entertained by his mistress?"

"I have the wrong accent," she said. "Surely you've noticed."

"I've noticed."

"Well, what shall I call *you*?"

"Call me Canute." He was grand and slightly drunk, she noticed.

"Why Canute?"

"Why not?" Later he had mentioned that it had to do with brooms, sweeping clean, witches, sweeping back the waves. When she protested that they were acting like children he agreed. They were giving themselves names, and therefore futures. Because they had no old names, they were free from the past, and history.

63

But not real futures, she protested. Only just-pretend futures, because they didn't have real names.

Seeg says Reality is calling things by their right names.

And X had a name which, of course, she later discovered in the dark when they were in bed together. And even before they went into the bedroom he apologized for having a wife and children and she said she didn't care, and she didn't.

X's name was so strong in her that whenever she thought of him she thought of him as X for fear she would speak to Seeg without thinking and say, "O, X darling?" or roll over in her sleep saying "X?"

When Seeg left for the office he turned away from her passionate kiss with an apology. It wasn't fair, he accused her gently, to start that when he had to leave. She had all day, endless time. He had to place himself on the market-block. She nodded and sent him off. If she weren't careful the day would begin sadly and uncomfortably.

She went at the apartment with an anger that was growing in her for being such a fool. In an hour it was cleaned, dusted, straightened. She tried to read a history of art criticism, but she couldn't. It bored her.

She had a cup of coffee for lunch, and took out her sketch-pad. She wished she had a canvas and a place to work. She would have liked to have caught that heavy green and quick yellow she had seen out the window in the morning. But canvas was too expensive for them right then. And the picture she imagined would be sloppy and sentimental. Might as well do landscapes and arrangements of fruit, she thought. Or hashed-up abstracts. Or nothing at all.

She took off her clothes to begin a drawing of herself, and sat cross-legged on the floor in front of the full-length mirror. She looked at herself seriously, turned this way and that, and decided she looked like a perfume advertisement. Seeg said that only naked people were real. Strip them bare.

She decided instead to do a drawing of her clothes, which were flung onto the chair. They seemed to form a vital arrangement against the chair's wooden order. The bra, for instance, seemed like a dead white bird brought in by a hunting husband. Her blouse, slip and skirt seemed to be abandoned. She concentrated on producing an adequate pencil-drawing.

The affair with X hadn't lasted long. But while it had, it was as if they were characters dancing through a film. Neither she nor X ever seemed to put a foot wrong, they never had an argument, and they delighted in the wantonness of letting their minds wander heedlessly. They could be gleefully stupid together. His long smile invited hers, and they tumbled into bed saying, "Let's trade skins."

They played out parts from novels they had read, and once had breakfast together in a hotel-room wearing nothing but the artificial flowers placed in the room for decoration. Another time she paraded around wearing X's heavy old cardigan, and he said, "That's obscene, take it off," and she did, button by button.

But then he had to leave when he said he had to leave, and with, "Reality now—one doesn't give up everything for love," he was gone quick as a knife. The film was over, there were bills to pay and livings to earn, and it was time to go home.

She remembered him by
  the scar on his back—motorcycle accident
  the lie he had told about the scar on his back, saying he got it in the Blitz
  the permanent blackhead in his cheek
  his ideas on the painting of Klee, which were naive
  his weight on her—
She pursed her lips and said his name to the mirror.

The drawing, she decided, was a rather good one. Pleasantly curious.

The evening turned grey and a gentle rain began to fall through the heavy green, stabilizing it. About supper-time Seeg called to say that he was going to join Figg (a comic failure, who spent his father's money) for a couple of beers at the Lord Beaverbrook Hotel. He spoke carefully because, though he wanted to tell her he would be home late, he didn't want to give the impression that he was asking permission. She was wary, also, because she didn't wish to appear possessive, and yet this was throwing her day off balance.

"I'll see you later, OK?"

"All right."

When he arrived home with a case of Ten-Penny ale under his arm he was fizzy with smiles and, as he said, ridiculously happy. He and Figg, he said, had spent a pleasant couple of hours telling lies to one another about success. "Always live in the past," he said, "because not only are you safe there—you are alive. The future is another matter."

His mood was boyish. He recounted Figg's great plan, to be called—ho-ho—*The Fig Market.* It was to be a supermarket for wives. For far too long the marriage market had been dominated by obscure economic policies, and whereas it was agreed that an open market and free trade were best, nonetheless, a little corporate organization would lead to a going concern. For example, he and Figg would simply work up a directory of all the eligible females in Fredericton, and then they would approach them, pointing out the benefits (financial and psychological) inherent in their plan. The women would present themselves on market day, and with him, Seeg, serving as auctioneer, they would be sold off to wooers.

"We'd begin by selling their clothes, of course. Fur coats, silk dresses, and so on. Gah! Can you imagine the price paid for the removal of a tender brassiere!" Seeg's face rolled with merriment.

"I'm afraid it's been done" she said.

"Ah, of course, of course."

"Slave markets of the east."

"Quite so."

"Marriage brokers."

"Yes. Of course. Nothing *new* about the plan except the commercial dream. Simply an institutionalizing of the present system of wooing. Lust is always made to pay," he said. "Ever notice how beautiful women are well-dressed?" He hurried on. "And since *most* women—I emphasize *most*, you note, for this sort of thing is for the great mindless classes—go into marriage for financial

66

security—see Ann Landers—why, it ought to work."

"I think you had a good time with Figg."

"I did, I confess. Good to get out with the boys now and again. I can see it now: the Great Fig Market: Original Sin and You Know What You're Paying For."

"The cosmic whorehouse," she said.

Seeg laughed. "With coloured lights and a band—why, it would be just like a wedding. You know, when I was a boy the newspapers always referred to whorehouses as 'bordellos.' I remember looking it up in the dictionary. It said it was a brothel. Then I looked that up. Never used a straightforward bare-assed word like cat-house or whore-house. Hah."

"But one term they used," he continued, "I never did figure out until they printed this story about the high-school girl who had an affair with the janitor and then killed him because of it. They asked her: 'Were you *in*timate with him,' and she said, 'Oh, yes.' And then they asked her, did she have sexual relations with him, which is what the old *News-Sun* meant by 'intimate,' and she swore stoutly that she had not. Now inasmuch as she was very much pregnant at the time, her answer was not given much credence, but she went off to jail swearing she'd never laid for the guy. In jail she said she wished she'd gone to Sunday School more, and she prayed a lot."

"Did it help?"

"Not so you could tell. She was a plump, chunky blonde."

He began to run down as he gradually sobered, and the talk drifted away. She prepared hamburgers for him which he swore were the best in the world, and afterwards he collapsed on the sofa. She watched TV, and he woke up and watched for a while.

She went to the bathroom and discovered that her period had begun and, feeling very silly, she fainted. Seeg came running and picked her up and was very concerned. He helped her into bed.

When he came to bed he said, "I liked the drawing you did today. It's really quite good. The best you've done."

She was pleased and thanked him.

"You're all right, aren't you?"

67

"Oh, yes. Just my period. I didn't eat enough today. I'm just tired, that's all."

In the close hot dark of the bed he was restless, and his voice came to her like the buzz of a fly.

"Look, if you ever want to leave me for somebody, you'll tell me, won't you?"

"Of course."

"And you don't have a lover."

"No, no," she said.

PITY THE POOR PIPER

D.O. Spettigue

If the girl got off here too that would be a sign. And she got off; but everyone got off. They were familiar with the stops and Shieling was a service-station lunchbar-depot stop.—Ten Minutes, the driver called, but they were not impressed. They would crowd into the lunchbar and the Ladies' and Men's, would wolf their hamburgs and burn their lips on the coffee and fifteen minutes later would sink into the stained green leather seats and wait for the driver to follow, glance down the row, fasten his ticket vendor, close the door at last—they all had their legs crossed and were huddled against the draught—and start the motor. Shortly the bus would be warm again and drowsy and silent, but for the rattle and roar—the people would be silent, the occasional whisper only, at first, and then they would stare out, and drowse. But now everyone got off the bus and crowded into the depot and the boy too with his little bag, but the girl—she wasn't alone after all; the kerchiefed woman with the basket from the seat in front must be her mother—simply got out and walked away.

The boy hesitated; when no-one offered any advice he walked across the packed snow past the gas pump, slowly because someone might ask to see his ticket stub though no-one did, then quickly to the sidewalk and away between banks of snow. The girl and her mother were gone and that was in a way a relief, though all the way here he had felt empty at the stomach just looking at her.

69

Not that she was anything, but that he was away from home, alone, riding up the peninsula by bus and there ought to be adventure in it for him. Adventure meant a girl, and she was the only one there.

Wearing a boyish brown jacket, her hair black and clipped short but the curve of the cheek surprisingly gentle and small; the jacket shapeless but in the warm bus half unzipped so that you could imagine your hand sliding into it and experiencing there the incredible softness of her breasts. But of course he hadn't spoken to her and there had been her mother and they had slipped away behind high sharp banks of snow.

The bus had come in on the highway that formed the cross of a T with the main road of the town. At the intersection a string of coloured lights still hung, unlit because it was Saturday afternoon a week after Christmas. A yellow caution light blinked in the centre. There was bustle about the stores down the street to the left, but the furniture warehouse on one corner was empty, and the houses thinned out along the highway. He crossed under the light. From the porch steps of the corner house a woman scattered salt on the walk. The boy asked where the Arthur house was. She turned her pail upside down and spanked the bottom sharply, then stood a moment, heavy and slow, before pointing a crusted hand.—Straight ahead. The grey frame at the next corner. That's old Mr. Arthur's. You likely want the perfesser though, dontcha? She stared from watery blue eyes.

—Do I? he said, I want Mr. Arthur the writer.

—That's the perfesser, she said. She considered. Well, it's near the end of the houses an it's an old yellow brick set back in. Mrs. Craig's likely there, she added. D'you know that?

He hadn't known that.

—Well, she's there. The woman turned away but looked once more at the spread of chilled slush that cracked and whispered at her feet.—She went down last night, she said, and went in.

A panel truck drew up at the sooty frame house before he reached it and he saw a frail bent old man open the door for the groceries. That's his father, he thought. And he doesn't know I'm passing his house on my way to see his son. His son is famous in his own town anyway, he thought. The Professor, because he wrote a book. And he likes my play, he thought. He invited me here because he liked what I showed him. And he pressed a hand against his overcoat to feel the bulk of the folded paper in the jacket pocket beneath.

The delivery truck leapfrogged ahead and across the street, completed its call and U-turned to the old yellow brick house opposite as the boy approached it. Though they were all much of an age as far as that went. Sixty years? Funny how the solid square brick houses in a little town could all look as if they were built the same day, not old, not new, but ageless. And how come the town could suddenly sprout them all and never grow another branch since? Like the black bare elms that lined the highway the length of the single residential street, all of a height though some had thicker trunks and some had split trunks and probably half of them were dead. Who planted them all at once and why didn't anyone plant any more? They stopped just beyond the yellow brick house. The driveway wasn't dug out and the truck remained at the street.

—Arthurs'? the delivery lad said. Right here. So the boy was gathered in with the groceries.

A grey, sharp woman let him in, then disappeared into the kitchen.

There was the warm smell of baking in the hallway. The parlour to the right was big and the fireplace lit and there was a large piano. A little girl rode a red tricycle in a circuit through the parlour and the hall. She had dark curly hair and big brown eyes and she wore a plaid skirt and black slippers.

—I missed my dancing lesson because I came home this morning, she said. I've been at Mrs. Craig's house for a whole week. I can dance the Highland Fling. Want to see me?

—Not now, Lucy, the housekeeper said. She took his hat and coat and set his boots on the mat. He didn't know how to talk to a little girl.

—Doesn't she look like her daddy? he said.

71

—You may do your dance for the gentleman while he's having a cup of tea and a hot buttered scone to warm him, the housekeeper said. You've come up by the bus, she said, as he followed her to the kitchen. Mr. Arthur will be down I think.

In his enthusiasm for the scones he could watch the slow gyrations of the child with some sympathy and could even applaud when the ritual ended.

—You're a pretty smart little girl, he said as Lucy repeated her curtsey.

—But is she beautiful? The familiar heavy masculine voice of Calvin Arthur; the darkly-shadowed face and deepset eyes of the familiar weekly column photo, but framed now in the kitchen doorway. Calvin Arthur wore a wine silk dressing gown. Under the shadow the face was faintly yellowed.

—Come change that skirt now, Lucy, the housekeeper said.

—Will she be beautiful? the father asked again. I couldn't stand to have a daughter who wasn't beautiful.

The boy smiled uneasily.

Calvin Arthur was a big man, his heavy body gone soft a little; his forehead was creased with thought, his eyes pouched from study and fatigue. He didn't look well but he fulfilled the image of gifted columnist and incisive critic.

—You didn't have difficulty finding me? He went ahead to the parlour.

—Oh no, the boy said.

—Did you ask for the Professor? If anybody wants to find me here he just has to ask for the Professor. That's the home-town term. Suddenly he smiled, and light irradiated. It wouldn't cut much ice in Toronto but in Shieling that's homage.

—Take the comfortable chair, he motioned. Shieling, Scots for a peasant's cottage. The reality of the old world is the romance of the new. Luce? he called suddenly. The child came in carrying a long wooden cigarette roller before her.

—How did you know I wanted that? He took it from her and inspected the paper and tobacco.

72

—Mrs. Craig said you would. The little girl was wearing jeans now.

—Dear Mrs. Craig, he said, thou hast delivered me out of the house of bondage, thou hadst compassion on mine affliction. The child marched out as solemnly as she had come.

Get them early and bring them up right, Calvin Arthur said.

He moved suddenly from the chair, stretched himself out on the blue carpet before the fireplace where a fire still smouldered in a maple block, and took up the cigarette roller. The boy watched him feed in the roll, spread the tobacco evenly, crank the cylinder and slice off the cigarettes. Abruptly the Professor asked, How's the great play? Finish it?

—I'm not sure, the boy said. I brought it anyway. He fumbled inside his jacket for the bundle of pages.

When I've rolled a few of these, Calvin Arthur said, I'll take it upstairs with me and read it through and then we can talk about it. You make yourself comfortable here, read anything you see at hand. There's a thing of mine there on the table, I thought it might do for *Chatelaine*. A bird's-eye view of the little town from the centre of the nest. He surveyed his makes critically, tapped each of them on the edge of the roller and set them one by one neatly into a wooden bowl.

—Do this for therapy, he said. Surprising how it relaxes. He pushed the bowl away abruptly, rolled on to his belly, put his hands behind his neck and strained with his neck muscles against his arms.

—Main thing is to relax the neck muscles, he panted.

The boy watched silently.

This is really it, he thought a moment later, listening to the heavy tread of the Professor up the stairs. I've been sitting here listening to him and him casually rolling homemades and doing exercises on the rug like a big friendly dog before the fire. And now he's got my play and he's gone upstairs to read it and I'm here just like home, trusted and—and liked. He tried to concentrate on the typescript. Bird's-eye view of Shieling: "Pshaw, the Doctor said." Did they still say pshaw in Shieling?

Like Shaw. He's reading my play. Will he like it? He can't like it, it's silly. But maybe he will like something in it I can't see. Like where Johnny sits alone in the mess, slumped over the keyboard and Myra sees him from the door and says to Mac, Find another strong back and get him to bed. Pity. But will he feel the pity? Pity the poor piano player. Can that flat dialogue convey love? Or the chess part. Will he think it's funny? A game at chess not of chess. Words Words Words.

Sounds. Lucy chattering in the kitchen. The boy walked restlessly about the room, looked at book covers, at the fire, at the wooden cigarette roller still on the blue carpet and the thin white cylinder in it. He went out to the kitchen, afraid of himself.

—You must be used to people coming to stay, he offered. The only reply was a grey immobility of face. My mother used to look disapproval that way, he thought. (Declines the gambit, shows fatigue.)

—Mrs. Craig and me don't stay here all the time, Lucy observed.

—Don't spill that, Lucy, the housekeeper said sharply. Here, we'll just tie on an apron so we won't spill on our clothes. The boy waited and watched her work, feeling alien and separate again. But the woman's disapproval struggled with something else and after a moment she said, He hasn't been well, you know.

—I didn't know.

—He sent for me just last night, this is the first day he's been up. If he is up, she muttered over the stove.

—I think he's reading a play of mine, the boy said, worried. I guess I shouldn't have come. I'm sorry, I didn't know he was sick.

—He has his spells, Mrs. Craig said softly. She turned half around from her baking, but not to look at him. He thinks he's going to die or something dreadful, he doesn't care, and he just lies in his bed and drinks his whisky. And it makes him sick. And he comes down here for milk and that's all he has, whisky and milk, until he runs out of the one or the milkman stops bringing the other for him not paying, or else he gets afraid himself of what he's doing, and Mercy knows it is a terrible thing, and then he sends

74

for me again and says Mrs. Craig, will you save me again? You've done it before, he says, I ask you to save me again.

—This little cup, Mrs. Craig? Lucy came over, showing a crockery mug. The housekeeper shook her head, took down a plastic tumbler and went to the counter where the child climbed again on her stool to play at work and they worked there together.

But sent for her how? By the milkman? By friends—were there other friends? And what kind of friends to let him do that to himself until he had to send, to beg, for this hard, generous old widow woman to come? Bird's-eye view of a little town. He ought to know. And the boy could sense the ripples circling outward from the big brick house through the town. But not beyond, eddying back again and never out beyond. The Professor has sent for Mrs. Craig again. Can't his father handle him, old Mr. Arthur? Hasn't the strength, isn't even asked. But did she go up to the big house herself last evening and talk to him? Has she been keeping Lucy all week, and does that almost empty house alone know what she said to him, what they said to one another? In the end he must have cried out to her for help and late in the winter day the lights would be turned out at Mrs. Craig's and then there would be lights in the kitchen and in the old bedroom downstairs at Calvin Arthur's and before bedtime all Shieling would know he had sent for Mrs. Craig again.

In the morning there would have been two milk bottles out, with money, and the steps, though not the drive, would be swept clear of fresh snow. Late in the morning Mrs. Craig herself would appear with the little girl walking around to the stores for shopping. She would bring back what she could carry with her and leave the rest of the groceries for—what had the name been on the truck?—for somebody's delivery, and on the way back would walk right past her own white frame cottage to the brick house that was Lucy's precarious home. So for lunch there would be the three of them there, though the Professor could not have come down. But the mailman— would Shieling have mail delivery? Someone might have picked up the mail for them at the Post Office, or Mrs. Craig might herself when she had been out, and into the centre of three would come his letter, the silly letter from a word-struck youth saying, "Dear Mr. Arthur, you said once I might come to Shieling so I dared. . . . " Mrs. Craig would wear that disapproving face of grey stoniness and would ask, What shall I do with him, Mr. Arthur? and the answer would be, out of pillows fluffed up at least now, and clean, from a mouth drawn wearily open and the eyes too, put him up, Mrs. Craig. The three would be four then, she would think. And others? All bringing trouble in their wake. What price glory? I shouldn't have come to bother him, the boy thought.

—C'n I help set the table? Lucy was asking.

—*May* I help, Mrs. Craig said severely. She was bending to slide a pan in and her voice came back from the oven. I don't know that we'll need to use the dining-room.

—I'll see if daddy's coming down. Lucy ran to the hall.

—No you won't. If daddy wants to come down he will. You can set the table here while I finish wiping up. Wait till I clear these off. Now then, the plates. And four butter plates. Can you get out four knives and four forks and four spoons? Little spoons.

—She must mean a great deal to him, the boy said.

But again there was the hard disapproval. Or only a conflict, the urge to veil and the urge to tell?

—Who looked after daddy when I was at your place? Lucy asked suddenly. She sat on the stool, selecting cutlery piece by piece from the drawer. I'm s'posed to look after him you know.

—We're both looking after him, Mrs. Craig said. You can help best by not bothering him.

—I wouldn't bozzer him, the child said. I would go ever so quiet up the stairs and I would peek in his room— first I would push open the door, gently . . . . She went on explaining to herself, nodding vigourously and waving a butter knife.

—She's not his child, you know. Somehow in telling it Mrs. Craig seemed to put the blame on the boy. He was struck silent. She said, they adopted her just a short

76

while before Marion died. It was a mistake. Marion, he thrilled. A real person. He hadn't supposed a real person attached to the black tie Calvin Arthur wore. I'm not saying, Mrs. Craig whispered, that he isn't fond of the child.

Bird's-eye view. Bird's nest. Jorrick's Jaunts and Jollities. Marion. I'm not saying he didn't love her. A toilet flushed and gurgled upstairs. Sick, then. Sick when? Had she been sick too: The two of them killing each other. Calvin and Marion. She wanting the child? Not saying he didn't love her. Eating his heart out now, then, and I bring him a manuscript.

What if he doesn't even read my manuscript?

Calvin Arthur didn't come down. Why doesn't daddy come down to dinner? Lucy asked repeatedly. He's doing some reading for Mr. Reid, the housekeeper said. Oh, me again. Spoiling their dinner. I won't stay overnight. I'll say I'm on my way through to—someplace. If he reads my play. Under Mrs. Craig's direction the boy made talk at the table. Lucy was going to school next fall. She was five. She had a friend Brenda. Brenda had a pony. I'm not saying he isn't fond of the child.

Lucy slept in the same room with Mrs. Craig. Calvin Arthur didn't appear until her bedtime; to raise her on his shoulders laughing that her fingers were in his eyes, and to carry her to her bedroom calling Goodnight Mrs. Craig, Goodnight Mr. Reid. Goodnight Lucy, the boy said. Mr. Arthur would read her a story, Mrs. Craig said. After a time his voice could be heard in the hallway reciting.

> Night, night, sleep tight
> Don't let the bugs bite.
> If they do, squeeze them tight
> And they won't come another night.

And a blown kiss, and Goodnight Lucy, and Calvin Arthur returned to the parlour. If he talked at once about the play that would mean he liked it. If he made small talk . . . . The boy's heart contracted. They sat in the parlour. Lucy had gone to sleep, Mrs. Craig had faded away, there was dim light and no fire.

Like that day in the Crocus Room Calvin Arthur had

ordered a drink for the boy and said to the barman, Jerry, here's a man writing the play of the year. Yeah? Jerry had said, blowing on a glass, saying nothing about his age. (So real barmen did blow on glasses. Part of the act?)

Calvin Arthur uncoiled from a deep black leather chair, paced to the window, stood beside the boy but looking out. Did you read my little bit for the ladies? he asked.

—It was very good, the boy said, and flushed. He had scarcely tasted the article while the great man, suffering who knew what sickness, had read his college play entire. But the Professor didn't wait for the response.

—Tucks right into them, doesn't it? Calvin Arthur's voice was big, too. He gloated. Did you get the Sister Helen type who uses her wax to singe the hair off her legs? Isn't that the real thing? Eh? And Mr. Peebles, the elder—mincing the words—"Don't you take even a little salt in your tomato juice, Miss Hume?" Eh? The real self underneath, Calvin Arthur said, and paced to his chair again.

—I see, the boy said.

—Now, your game of chess bit, Calvin Arthur said, the old fellow and the girl getting more and more nervous, atmosphere building up around them as they play. All right, tension, suspense, trying to keep the lid on. But a chess game! Old hat, Dicky. Old, old hat.

The familiar name caught at his ear and again the boy's heart contracted. He was being let down nicely. Almost too nicely; he couldn't bear it. How to fill up the hours till sleep, how to make talk interesting enough that the critic wouldn't yawn in his face, when there was no play left between them. I can't bear it if he tries to pretend I could still make a play of it, he thought. I don't want to hear about the play again.

—Smoke? Calvin Arthur jumped to his feet, seized the wooden bowl of cigarettes and offered it to the boy.

—No, the boy said. No thank you.

—Neither do I, said his host. Just trying you. He dropped the bowl onto an end table and stood again—nervously?—at the window.

—There is a boy, he said, and ruminated. I expect

78

you'll see him. A lovely boy. I expect he'll drop in tonight.

Dick couldn't see past him at the window. Oh? he said.

—He usually comes Saturday nights, Calvin Arthur said. I'd like you to meet him. Name of Roberts, Malcolm Roberts; his father's the town's favourite preacher, rampant old Grit and New Light. Malcolm's a bright lad, a fine lad, really a lovely boy. You'll see, you'll meet him. He won't say much; he's shy, like you, only worse. Much worse. Malcolm's—he swung away from the window—afraid; he's afraid to be himself. Too much personality on the father's part, nothing left for the son, no little area where Malcolm could be himself, no way to compensate for his father. So he went inside, you know. The buried life. He's been in the Ontario Hospital— Calvin Arthur striding about the room now, piano, red rug, blue rug, vacant fireplace, bowl of homemades on the end table, back again to the red rug. He tried to kill his father once, with a hockey stick. It was supposed to be an accident, but he told me the real story himself. He's home now, he's back. You'll see him. He comes over—

Mrs. Craig stood in the parlour doorway, in white frilled night net and faded blue kimono. I wondered if you and the gentleman wanted me to put on milk to warm before bed, Mr. Arthur, she said.

—Good for the tummy, Dick, Calvin Arthur said heartily. Thank you, Mrs. Craig, we do. And two or three of your scones apiece with crabapple jelly. Your scones have made a hit with our guest. He winked at Richard Reid. He had a wide mouth and his jaws showed black when he laughed.

It was a big house. The upstairs hall had bedrooms off either side and the bathroom at the end. Mrs. Craig had put Richard's bag in the first room at the head of the stairs. She turned on the light and told him to draw up the comforter if he needed it. Mr. Arthur usually sleeps late Sunday mornings, she added, but Lucy and I will be in the kitchen when you come down.

He thanked her and waited until she had gone down

the stairs before he began to undress. He heard Calvin Arthur on the stairs say, I'll read in bed a while, Mrs. Craig. Don't mind me. Richard shut his door silently. He waited for stillness throughout the house before he would go along to the bathroom, but the naked bulb still burned in the hall. His room was a country bedroom with crossed frilled curtains on the window, a deep feather tick, bosomy comforter to pull up against his cheek. If he had just read the article and said something casual about it, something brilliant. If he hadn't been there under false pretences. If only the play had been good.

The bedroom door pushed open silently and Calvin Arthur in pyjamas stood in the white wedge of light from the hall. Richard sat up and hugged his knees and said Come in, embarrassedly.

Calvin Arthur padded to the point of the white wedge and said, I'm sorry, I hadn't realized you were bedded down for the night. I was just going to suggest we talk a bit. But it's nothing that can't wait till morning if you prefer.

—Of course not, Richard said. I wasn't sleepy.

—I hope I didn't offend you over the play, Calvin Arthur said. I didn't mean that it was all that bad, you know, but I thought it was better to . . . .

—Oh no, Richard burst out. Of course I wasn't offended. I mean it was so good of you to—

He hesitated, confused. Calvin Arthur stood there in pyjamas, his bare toes curling up from the floor. Good heavens! he said, this wasn't hospitality. We gave you the only bedroom without any rug. He stepped from the light to the dark patch of floor near the bed.

—Oh, Richard said, startled. I didn't think. Sit up on the bed, of course! He felt himself flushed. Ought he to get up? The tent and the camel, but it could hardly be.

—Only if you're sure you wouldn't rather sleep, Calvin Arthur said. He lifted a buttock onto the bed, leaned on his fists and slid himself back. The boy drew his knees up closer.

—I'm sorry, I didn't think, he murmured.

Calvin Arthur gathered his own knees to his chest and smiled. His eyes sank in their pouches, his mouth moving in shadow. You mustn't say it was good of me to read your play, he explained patiently and quietly as to a child, because the reading is nothing compared with the feeling behind it. You will write other plays. It isn't your writing I'm interested in, it's you. You as a person.

He stretched out beside the boy, raised himself, slipped up the covers and slid in beside him. That's better, he said.

But for the boy it was chaos. Richard stared straight up at the blank ceiling and the wedge of light. Ah, wilderness!

—When I first suggested to you that you might come here, Calvin Arthur said, I had in mind you as the lost soul I have found in your writing, the lonely creator, and I could visualize your soul reaching out to mine in sympathy, a kind of creative act between us, a coming together in perfect friendship with nothing sordid, nothing of the taint of the outside world, money and banking and the critical knife, only true creative friendship. He paused.

My play, the boy thought, my play. He doesn't care about my play.

—Does this frighten you? Calvin Arthur asked in a new tone, ironical. Does it surprise you to find there are other lonely people in the world? In the silence he wrapped a strong arm about the boy and held him close. Odour of man and clean sheets and faintly fresh tobacco. Are you frightened, Dicky? he asked.

—I guess so, Richard said. His voice was hoarse. He didn't know what he felt—horror? He was rigid.

—It's funny, isn't it? Calvin Arthur said, that two people can be as close friends as we are, so involved with each other that you would come all this way by bus to give us a weekend together, and yet be afraid to admit our affection, afraid to put our arms around each other. (Jonathan and David were lovely and pleasant in their lives and in death they were not divided.) Why are you afraid of me, Dicky? he asked. Would you be afraid to let your mother or father embrace you? He drew the boy closer. Relax, he said. Try to relax. But the boy only stiffened further, and began now to draw away to the edge of the bed. —Don't, he choked.

Calvin Arthur rolled back a little on his elbow and a

movement in the shadow may have been a smile on his face, but his voice was cutting.

—Very interesting, he said. I wondered how the experiment would go. You were rigid, of course, but not as rigid as I might have expected.

Experiment. Putting it on to me again, making me bear the guilt, the doubt. What did it mean? Richard couldn't think. The pain of being so young! I don't mean to say he isn't fond of the child.

Calvin Arthur slipped his feet out and stood up. Out of darkness he said, meanly. Too bad about the play, and at the door again he said, Goodnight, Dicky, but his voice wasn't kind.

Mephistopheles! But he didn't understand.

Richard summoned a tattered dignity. Don't call me Dicky, he said.

He came down haggard in the morning when he heard Lucy and Mrs. Craig in the kitchen. He brought his bag with him and set it near the kitchen door. There was porridge waiting, and then there was toast and tea, and crabapple jelly. Richard was surprised to find he was hungry; it didn't seem right. Mrs. Craig was sour, almost hostile to him. Once he tempted her, exasperated, with Why does that man drink? but she didn't answer him. Lucy chattered all through breakfast. She was going to wear her plaid skirt to Sunday School. She had a rag doll. Upstairs there was walking, a toilet flushing, a door.

—I won't be here for lunch, the boy told her resolutely. I think I'll leave now. No answer. Steps on the stair. He waited in the kitchen. Steps in the hall and parlour. Voices.

—I have to go now, Richard said. Thank you. I did like your scones, Mrs. Craig. Goodbye Lucy, he said. The child stared solemnly.

He took his bag and went to the front door for his coat and boots. Calvin Arthur came out of the parlour.

—Oh, Richard, he said, I'd like you to meet a neighbour, Malcolm Roberts. Malcolm, Richard Reid, a literary acquaintance of mine.

Confusion. He—they—must have come down as he

had made his farewells with Mrs. Craig and Lucy. The boys scarcely exchanged glances as they met. Malcolm had colourless eyes, fair hair. His hand was warm and wet.

Richard muttered Hello and retreated to the door. One moment, Calvin Arthur said to his second guest, and opened the door himself. Lovely morning, he said. He must know, Richard thought, that it's hours till the bus goes yet.

It was a bright brisk morning. A sifting of fresh snow glittered on the walk, on the umbrella ribs of austere elms, glittered between the tire paths on the morning highway. Richard walked quickly away from the house, almost ran along the sidewalk. He passed the father's house, the grey frame set back from the street, silent in the Sunday morning. His son's house a block back now, near the end of the timeless elms, solid, faded, yellow brick. Circles beat out from that centre, expanded in the boy's mind. At the intersection the coloured lights still hung stiff, unlit; the orange caution light blinked steadily, blindly, on desolation. Glittering banks of snow. He would stand outside the depot for hours yet stamping off the cold. Some two or three would see. Just ask for the Professor. My play, my play. Circles widened. Pity the poor piper.

A day or two and Mrs. Craig would leave again, and Lucy with her, or with her grandfather, and the big house would be almost empty again and silent, but for deliveries. And every now and again a visitor for the Professor. And would the village swell with pride? Until the deliveries stopped again, the boy thought, and word went about again, and they sent again for Mrs. Craig.

At ten the depot opened and he had coffee. It would be safer in the bus and, once the doors were closed, warmer.

THE MILITARY HOSPITAL

Phyllis Gotlieb

The helicopter moved through the city in the airlane between skyscrapers. It was on autopilot, preset course, and there was no-one to squint down the canyons of the streets where the life-mass seethed. Children looked up at it with dull eyes; if it had come lower they would have stoned or shot at it. The armoured cars that burrowed among them were scratched and pocked from their attacks.

Fresh and smooth, dressed in crisp white, DeLazzari came into the Control Room at the top of the Hospital. He had had a week off, he was on for three; he ran the Hospital, supervised nurse-patient relationships, directed the sweepers in the maintenance of sterility, and monitored the pile. He took over this function wherever he was told to go, but he particularly liked the Military Hospital because it was clean, roomy, and had very few patients. He was a stocky man with thick black hair, broad wings of moustache, and skin the colour of baked earth; he had the blood of all nations in him. "The bad blood of all nations," he would add with a laugh if he felt like impressing one of the trots Mama Rakosy sent up to the apartment, though it was rare he felt like impressing anyone. He was sworn to forego women, drugs and liquor for three weeks, so he switched on the big external screen and dumped out of his bag the cigars, candy and gum that would sustain him, while he watched the course of the helicopter over the city.

A trasher's bomb went off in one of the buildings; daggers of glass blew out singing, and sliced at the scalps and shoulders of a knot of demonstrators clumped at its base; a fragment of concrete hurled outward and grazed the helicopter, then fell to dent a fibreglass helmet and concuss the bike-rider who fell from his machine and lay unconscious under the bruising feet; the wounded demonstrators scattered or crawled, leaving their placards, and others took their places, raising neon-coloured cold-light standards of complicated symbols; they camped in the table-sized space, oblivious to bloody glass, hardhats with crossbows, skinheads with slingshots, longhairs, freaks, mohicans, children, and above all the whoop and howl of police sirens coming up.

The helicopter moved north and away; the armoured cars butted their way through, into less crowded streets where merchants did business across wickets in iron cages in which one touch of a floor button dropped steel shutters and made a place impregnable fast enough to cut a slice off anyone who got in the way. Farther north the City Hospital and the Central Police Depot formed two wings of a great moth-shaped complex webbed about by stalled paddy-wagons and ambulances.

DeLazzari grinned. In City Hospital twelve Directors manned the Control Room, endlessly profane and harried. Shop was always depleted: the sweepers rusted and ground down from lack of parts and the nurses were obsolete and inefficient. Only the Doctors moved at great speed and in Olympian calm.

He switched on his own O.R. screen. Doctors were already closing round the operating table, waiting. They were silver, slab-shaped, featureless. They drew power from a remote source, and nobody he knew had any idea where it was. They had orders and carried them out—or perhaps they simply did what they chose. He had never been in their physical presence, nor wanted to be.

The helicopter was passing between blank-walled buildings where the dead were stored in very small vaults, tier upon tier upon tier; at street level the niches reserved for floral tributes were empty except for wire frames to which a few dried leaves and petals clung trembling in

85

the down draft from the rotors. North beyond that in the concrete plaza the racers were heating up for the evening, a horde endlessly circling.

But the city had to end in the north at the great circle enclosing the Military Hospital. It had no wall, no road, no entrance at ground level. What it had was a force-field the helicopter had to rise steeply to surmount. Within, for a wall it had a thicket of greenery half a mile deep going all the way round; outside the field there was a circuit of tumbled masonry pieces, stones, burnt sticks, as if many ragged armies had tried to storm it and retreated, disgusted and weary.

Inside there was no great mystery. The Military Hospital healed broken soldiers from distant and ancient wars; the big circular building had taken no architectural prizes, and on its rolling greens two or three stumbling patients were being supported on their rounds by nurses. Like all Directors DeLazzari tended to make himself out a minor Dracula; like all the rest his power lay in the modicum of choice he had among the buttons he pushed.

The helicopter landed on its field and discharged its cell, a Life Unit in which a dying soldier lay enmeshed; it took on another cell, containing another soldier who had been pronounced cured and would be discharged germ-free into his theatre of war; it was also boarded by the previous Director, pocket full of credits and head full of plans for a good week.

The Hospital doors opened. the cell rolled through them down a hall into an ante-room where it split, a wagon emerged from it carrying the patient and his humming, flickering life-system, the ante-room sealed itself, flooded with aseptic sprays and drained, washing away blood-traces; the O.R. sweeper removed the wet packs from the ruined flesh and dropped them on the floor, which dissolved them. In the operating room the TV system was pumping, the monitors pulsed, the Doctors activated their autoclaves in one incandescent flash and then extruded a hundred tentacles, probes, knives, sensors, and flexed them; their glitter and flash was almost blinding in the harsh light. DeLazzari was obliged to watch them; he hated it, and they needed no light. It was provided on demand of the Supervisors' and Directors' Union, though if machines chose to go renegade there was very little the Supervisors and Directors could say or do.

Doctors had never gone renegade. Neither had sweepers or nurses; it was a delicious myth citizens loved to terrify themselves with, perhaps because they resented the fact that madness should be reserved for people. DeLazzari thought that was pretty funny and he was scared too.

The O.R. sweeper sprayed himself (DeLazzari thought of it as delousing), the doors opened, the sweeper pushed in the body, still housing its low flicker of life, removed the attachments and set it on the table. The Doctors reattached what was needed; the sweeper backed into a corner and turned his own power down. DeLazzari flicked a glance at the indicator and found it correct.

One Doctor swabbed the body with a personal nozzle and began to remove steel fragments from belly and groin, another slit the chest and reached in to remove bone slivers from the left lung, a third trimmed the stump of the right forefinger and fitted a new one from the Parts Bank, a fourth tied off and removed torn veins from the thighs, all without bumping head shoulders or elbows because they had none, a fifth kept the throat clear, a sixth gave heart massage, the first opened the belly and cut out a gangrened bowel section, the third sewed and sealed the new right forefinger and as an afterthought trimmed the nail, the fifth, still watching every breath, peeled back sections of the scalp and drilled holes in the skull. All in silence except for the soft clash and ringing of sensors, knives and probes. Blood splashed; their body surfaces repelled it in a mist of droplets and the floor washed it away.

The sweeper turned his power up on some silent order and fetched a strange small cage of silver wires. The fifth Doctor took it, placed it over the soldier's head, and studied its nodes as co-ordinates in relation to the skull. Then he spoke at last. "Awaken," he said.

DeLazzari gave a hoarse nervous laugh and whispered, *Let there be light.* The boy's eyelids flickered and opened. The eyes were deep blue; the enlarged pupils contracted promptly and at an equal rate. DeLazzari wondered, as always, if he were conscious enough to be afraid he was lying in an old cemetery among the gravestones. Silver graves.

"Are you awake?" The voice was deep, God-the-Father-All-Powerful. The Doctor checked the nose tube and cleared the throat. "Max, are you awake?"

"Yes . . . yes . . . yes . . . . "

"Can you answer questions?"

"Yes."

"Recording for psychiatric report." He extruded a fine probe and inserted it into the brain. "What do you see? Tell me what you see."

"I see . . . from the top of the ferris wheel I can see all the boats in the harbour, and when I come down in a swoop all the people looking up . . . . "

The probe withdrew and re-entered. "What do you see now, Max?"

"My father says they're not sweet peas but a wild-flower, like a wild cousin of the sweet pea, toadflax, some people call them butter-and-eggs . . . . 'Scrophulariaceae Linaria vulgaris is the big name for them, Max, and that vulgaris means common, but they're not so common any more . . . . ' "

Probe.

" . . . something like the fireworks I used to watch when I was a kid, but they're not fireworks, they're the real thing, and they turn the sky on fire . . . . "

"Area established."

Probe.

"One eye a black hole and the kid lying across her with its skull, with its skull, with its skull, I said Chrissake, Yvon, why'd you have to? Yvon? why'd you have to? why? he said ohmigod Max how was I to know whether they were? Max? how was I to know whether?"

The probe tip burned, briefly.

"Yes, Max? He said: how was I to know whether what?"

"Know what? Who's he? I don't know what you're talking about."

DeLazzari watched the probes insinuate the cortex and withdraw. The Doctors pulled at the associations, unravelling a tangled skein; they didn't try to undo all the knots, only the most complicated and disturbing. Was the act, he wondered, a healing beneficence or a removal of guilt associated with killing?

After four or five burns the cage was removed and the scalp repaired. Surprised, Delazzari punched O.R. Procedures, Psych Division, and typed:

WHY SURGEONS OMIT DEEP MIL. INDOCTRINATION?

NEW RULING ONE WEEK PREVIOUS, the computer said.

WHOSE AUTHORITY?

BOARD OF SUPERVISORS.

And who ordered them around? He switched off and turned back to the Doctors.

After their duties had been completed they followed some mysteriously-developed ritual that looked like a laying on of hands. All probes and sensors extended, they would go over a body like a fine-tooth comb, slicing off a wart, excising a precancerous mole, straightening a twisted septum. DeLazzari switched off and lit a cigar. There were no emergencies to be expected in the next ten minutes. He blinked idly at a small screen recording the flat encephalogram of a dead brain whose body was being maintained for Parts.

The Doctors had other customs that both annoyed and amused him by their irrationality. Tonight they had been quiet, but sometimes one of them, sectioning a bowel, might start a running blue streak of chatter like a Las Vegas comic while another, probing the forebrain, would burst out in a mighty organ baritone, "Nearer My God To Thee." On the rare but inevitable occasions when an irreparable patient died with finality they acted as one to shut down the life system and retract their instruments; then stood for five minutes in a guardian circle of quietness, like the great slabs of Stonehenge, around the body before they would allow the sweeper to take it away.

The big external screen was still on and DeLazzari looked down into the city, where a torchlight procession was pushing its flaming way up the avenue and the walls to either side wavered with unearthly shadows. He shut off and called Shop. He peered at the fax sheet on Max Vingo clipped to his notice-board and typed:

YOU GOT A CAUCASIAN TYPE NURSE APPROX FIVE-SEVEN FAIR HAIR QUIET VOICE NOT PUSHY MILD-TO-WARM AND FIRST RATE?

2482 BEST QUALITY CHECKED OUT LIGHT BROWN WE CAN MAKE IT FAIR HAIR.

LIGHT BROWN OK HEALING UNIT 35.

He yawned. Nothing more for the moment. He dialled supper, surveyed the sleeping-alcove and bathroom, all his own, with satisfaction, checked the pill dispenser which allowed him two headache tablets on request, one sleeping pill at 11 PM and one laxative at 7.30 AM if required. He was perfectly content.

All nurses looked about twenty-five years old, unutterably competent but not intimidating unless some little-boy type needed a mother. 2482 was there when Max Vingo first opened his eyes and stirred weakly in his mummy-wrappings.

"Hello," she said quietly.

He swallowed; his throat was still sore from the respirator. "I'm alive."

"Yes, you are, and we're glad to have you."

"This is a hospital."

"It is, and I'm your nurse, 2482."

He stared at her. "You're a—a mechanical—I've heard about you—you're a mechanical—"

"I'm a Robonurse," she said.

"Huh . . . it sounds like some kind of a tank."

"That's a joke, baby—God help us," said DeLazzari, and turned her dial up half a point.

She smiled. "I'm not at all like a tank."

"No." He gave it a small interval of thought. "No, not at all."

It was the third day. DeLazzari never bothered to shave or wash on duty where he didn't see another human being; his face was covered with grey-flecked stubble. Outside he was vain, but here he never glanced into a mirror. The place was quiet; no new patients had come in, no alarms had sounded, the walking wounded were walking by themselves. Besides 2482 there were only two other nurses on duty, one with a nephritis and another tending the body soon to be frozen for Parts. Still, he did have 2482 to control and he watched with weary amusement as she warmed up under the turn of his dial.

"You're getting better already." She touched Max Vingo's forehead, a non-medical gesture since the thermocouple already registered his temperature. Her fingers were as warm as his skin. "You need more rest. Sleep now." Narcotic opened into his bloodstream from an embedded tube, and he slept.

On the fifth day the people of the city rose up against their government and it fell before them. Officers elected themselves, curfews were established, the torchlight parades and demonstrations stopped; occasionally a stray bomb exploded in a callbox. Packs of dogs swarmed up the avenue, pausing to sniff at places where the blood had lain in puddles; sometimes they met a congregation of cats and there were snarling yelping skirmishes. DeLazzari eyed them on his screen, devoutly thankful that he was not stationed in City Hospital. He filled City's requests for blood, plasma and parts as far as regulations required and didn't try to contact their Control Room.

At the Military Hospital the nephritis got up and walked out whole, the deadhead was cut up and frozen in Parts, an interesting new malaria mutation came in and was assigned a doctor to himself in Isolation. 2482 peeled away the bandages from Max Vingo's head and hand.

He asked for a mirror and when she held it before him he examined the scars visible on his forehead and scalp and said, "I feel like I'm made up of spare parts." He lifted his hand and flexed it. "That's not so funny." The forefinger was his own now, but it had once belonged to a black man and though most of the pigment had been chemically removed it still had an odd bluish tinge. "I guess it's better than being without one."

91

"You'll soon be your old handsome self."

"I bet you say that to all the formerly handsome guys."

"Of course. How would you get well otherwise?"

He laughed, and while she was wiping his face with a soft cloth he said, "2482, haven't you ever had a name?"

"I've never needed one."

"I guess if I get really familiar I can call you 2 for short."

"Hoo boy, this is a humourist." DeLazzari checked the dial and indicator and left them steady on for the while. The malaria case went into convulsions without notice and he turned his attention elsewhere.

She rubbed his scalp with a cream to quicken regrowth of hair.

"What does that do for a bald guy?"

"Nothing. His follicles no longer function."

He flexed his new finger again and rubbed the strange skin with the fingertips of his other hand. "I hope mine haven't died on me."

By day 7 DeLazzari was beginning to look like a debauched beachcomber. His hospital whites were grimy and his moustache ragged. However, he kept a clean desk, his sweeper cleared away the cigar stubs and the ventilators cleaned the air. Two badly-scarred cases of yaws came in from a tropical battleground and two Doctors called for skin grafts and whetted their knives. In the city a curfew violator was shot and killed, and next morning the first of the new demonstrators appeared. One of the Doctors took the chance of visiting Max for the first time when he was awake.

The soldier wasn't dismayed; he answered questions readily enough, showed off his growing hair, and demonstrated his attempts to use the grafted finger, but he kept looking from the Doctor to 2482 and back in an unsettling way, and DeLazzari turned up the nurse's dial a point.

When the Doctor was gone she said, "Did he disturb you?"

"No." But his eyes were fixed on her.

92

She took his hand. "Does that feel good?"

"Yes," he said. "That feels good." And he put his other hand on top of hers.

DeLazzari ate and slept and monitored the screens and supervised the duties of nurses and sweepers. Sometimes he wiped his oily face with a tissue and briefly considered rationing his cigars, which he had been smoking excessively because of boredom. Then three cases of cholera came in from the east; one was dead on arrival and immediately incinerated, the other two occupied him. But he still had time to watch the cure of Max Vingo and by turns of the dial nourish his relationship with 2482. He thought they were a pretty couple.

Max got unhooked from his TV, ate solid food with a good appetite and got up and walked stiffly on his scarred legs, now freed of their bandages. His hair grew in, black as DeLazzari's but finer, and the marks on his skin were almost invisible. He played chess sometimes with 2482 and didn't make any comments when she let him win. But there was an odd sadness about him, more than DeLazzari might have guessed from his Psych report. Although the ugliest of his memories had been burned away the constellations of emotion attached to them had remained and the Doctors would never be able to do anything about those during the short time he stayed in the Hospital.

So that often at night, even sometimes when he fell into a light doze, he had sourceless nightmares he couldn't describe, and when he flailed his arms in terrified frustration 2482 took his hands and held them in her own until he slept at peace.

DeLazzari watched the TV news, followed the courses of battles over the world and on Moonbase and Marsport, and made book with himself on where his next casualties would be coming from. Not from the planets, which had their own Hospitals, or from the usual Military Base establishments. His own Hospital (he liked to think of it as his own because he was so fond of its conveniences and so full of respect for its equipment) was one of the rare few that dealt with the unusual, the interesting and the hopeless. Down in the city the fire marchers were out and the bombs were exploding again. He knew that soon once more the people of the city would rise against their government and it would fall before them, and he kept check of blood and parts and ordered repairs on old scuppered nurses.

Max Vingo dressed himself now and saw the scars fade on his newly-exposed torso. Because he was so far away from it he didn't think of the battle he might be going into. It was when he had stood for a long time at the window looking out at the rain, at how much greener it made the grass, that 2482 said to him, "Max, is there something you're afraid of?"
"I don't know."
"Is it the fighting?"
"I don't even remember much of that."
"The Doctors took those memories away from you."

"Hey!" DeLazzari growled, hand poised over the control. "Who said you could say a thing like that?"

"I don't mind that," Max said.

DeLazzari relaxed.

"Don't you want to know why?"
"If you want to tell me."
"I'm not sure ... but I think it was because the Doctors knew you were a gentle and loving man, and they didn't want for you to be changed."
He turned and faced her. "I'm the same. But I'm still a man who has to dress up like a soldier—and I don't know when that will ever change. Maybe that's why I'm frightened."

DeLazzari wondered for a moment what it would be like to be sick and helpless and taken care of by a loving machine in the shape of a beautiful woman. Then he

94

laughed his hoarse derisive crow and went back to work. He had never been sick.

On the eighteenth day five poison cases came in from a bloodless coup in a banana republic; DeLazzari sent a dozen nurses with them into the Shock Room and watched every move. He was hot and itchy, red-eyed and out of cigars, and thinking he might as well have been in City Hospital. They were having their troubles over there, and once again he sent out the supplies. By the time he had leisure for a good look at Max Vingo, 2482's dial was all the way up and Max was cured and would be going out next day: day 21, his own discharge date. He listened to their conversation for a while and whistled through his teeth. "End of a beautiful interlude," he said.

That evening Max ate little and was listless and depressed. 2482 didn't press him to eat or speak, nor did DeLazzari worry. The behaviour pattern was normal for situation and temperament.

Max went to sleep early but woke about eleven and lay in the darkness without calling or crying out, only stared toward the ceiling; sometimes for a moment he had a fit of trembling.

2482 came into the room softly, without turning on the light. "Max, you're disturbed."

"How do you know?" he said in an expressionless voice.

"I watch your heartbeat and your brainwaves. Are you feeling ill?"

"No."

"Then what is the matter? Do you have terrible thoughts?"

"It's the thoughts I can't think that bother me, what's behind everything that got burned away. Maybe they shouldn't have done that, maybe they should have let me become another person, maybe if I knew, really knew, really knew what it was like to hurt and kill and be hurt and be killed and live in filth for a lifetime and another lifetime, ten times over, I'd get to laugh at it and like it and say it was the way to be, the only way to be and the way I should have been . . . . "

95

"Oh no, Max. No, Max. I don't believe so."

Suddenly he folded his arms over his face and burst out weeping, in ugly tearing sobs.

"Don't, Max." She sat down beside him and pulled his arms away. "No, Max. Please don't." She pulled apart the fastenings of her blouse and clasped his head between her tender, pulsing and unfleshly breasts.

DeLazzari grinned lasciviously and watched them on the infrared scanner, chin propped on his hand. "Lovely, lovely, lovely," he whispered. Then he preset 2482's dial to move down three points during the next four hours, popped his pill and went to bed.

The alarm woke him at four. "Now what in hell is that?" He staggered groggily over to the console to find the source. He switched on lights. The red warning signal was on over 2482's dial. Neither the dial nor the indicator had moved from UP position. He turned on Max Vingo's screen. She had lain down on the bed beside him and he was sleeping peacefully in her arms. DeLazzari snarled. "Circuit failure." The emergency panel checked out red in her number. He dialled Shop.

REROUTE CONTROL ON 2482.

CONTROL REROUTED, the machine typed back.

WHY DID YOU NOT REROUTE ON AUTO WHEN FAILURE REGISTERED?

REGULATION STATES DIRECTOR AUTONOMOUS IN ALL ASPECTS NURSE-PATIENT RELATIONSHIP NOW ALSO IN-CLUDING ALTERNATE CIRCUITS.

WHY WAS I NOT TOLD THAT BEFORE?

THAT IS NEW REGULATION. WHY DO YOU NOT REQUEST LIST OF NEW REGULATIONS DAILY UPDATED AND READILY AVAILABLE ALL TIMES?

"At four o'clock in the morning?" DeLazzari punched off. He noted that the indicator was falling now, and on the screen he could see 2482 moving herself away from Max and smoothing the covers neatly over him.

DeLazzari woke early on the last day and checked out the cholera, the yaws and the poison. The choleras were nearly well; one of the yaws needed further work on palate deformity; one of the poisons had died irrevocably, he sent it to Autopsy; another was being maintained in Shock, the rest recovering.

While he ate breakfast he watched the news of battle and outrage; growing from his harshly uprooted childhood faith a tendril of thought suggested that Satan was plunging poisoned knives in the sores of the world. "DeLazzari the Metaphysician!" He laughed. "Go on, you bastards, fight! I need the work." The city seemed to be doing his will, because it was as it had been.

Max Vingo was bathing himself, depilating his own face, dressing himself in a new uniform. A sweeper brought him breakfast. DeLazzari, recording his Director's Report, noted that he seemed calm and rested, and permitted himself a small glow of satisfaction at a good job nearly finished.

When the breakfast tray was removed, Max stood up and looked around the room as if there was something he might take with him, but he had no possessions. 2482 came in and stood by the door.

"I was waiting for you," he said.

"I've been occupied."

"I understand. It's time to go, I guess."

"Good luck."

"I've had that already." He picked up his cap and looked at it. "2482—Nurse, may I kiss you?"

DeLazzari gave her the last downturn of the dial.

She stared at him and said firmly, "I'm a machine, sir. You wouldn't want to kiss a machine." She opened the top of her blouse, placed her hands on her chest at the base of her neck and pulled them apart, her skin opened like a seam. Inside she was the gold and silver gleam of a hundred metals threaded in loops, wound on spindles, flickering in minute gears and casings; her workings were almost fearsomely beautiful, but she was not a woman.

"Get's 'em every time." DeLazzari yawned and waited for the hurt shock, the outrage, the film of hardness coming down over the eyes like a third eyelid.

Max Vingo stood looking at her in her frozen posture of display. His eyelids twitched once, then he smiled. "I would have been very pleased and grateful to kiss a machine," he said and touched her arm lightly. "Goodbye, Nurse." He went out and down the hall toward his transportation cell.

DeLazzari's brows rose. "At least that's a change." 2482 was still standing there with her innards hanging out. "Close it up, woman. That's indecent." For a wild moment he wondered if there might be an expression trapped behind her eyes, and shook his head. He called down Shop and sent her for post-patient diagnostic with special attention to control system.

He cleaned up for the new man. That is, he evened up the pile of tape reels and ate the last piece of candy. Then he filched an ID plate belonging to one of the poison cases, put everything on AUTO, went down a couple of floors and used the ID to get into Patients' Autobath. For this experience of hot lather, stinging spray, perfume and powder he had been saving himself like a virgin.

When he came out in half an hour he was smooth, sweet-smelling and crisply clothed. As the door locked behind him five Doctors rounded a corner and came down the corridor in single file. DeLazzari stood very still. Instead of passing him they turned with a soft whirr of their lucite castors and came near. He breathed faster. They formed a semicircle around him; they were featureless and silver, and smelt faintly of warm metal. He coughed.

"What do you want?"

They were silent.

"What do you want, hey? Why don't you say something?"

They came nearer and he shrank against the door, but there were more machines on the other side.

"Get away from me! I'm not one of your stinking zombies!"

The central Doctor extruded a sensor, a slender shining limb with a small bright bulb on the end. It was harmless, he had seen it used thousands of times from the

Control Room, but he went rigid and broke out into a sweat. The bulb touched him very lightly on the forehead, lingered a moment, and retracted. The Doctors, having been answered whatever question they had asked themselves, backed away, resumed their file formation, and went on down the hall. DeLazzari burst into hoarse laughter and scrubbed with his balled fist at the place the thing had touched. He choked on his own spit, sobered after a minute, and walked away very quickly in the opposite direction, even though it was a long way around to where he wanted to go. Much later he realized that they had simply been curious and perplexed in the presence of an unfamiliar heartbeat.

He went out in the same helicopter as Max Vingo, though the soldier in his sterile perimeter didn't know that. In the Control Room the new Director, setting out his tooth-cleaner, depilatory and changes of underwear, watched them on the monitor. Two incoming helicopters passed them on the way; the city teemed with fires and shouting and the children kicked at the slow-moving cars. In the operating theatre the silver Doctors moved forward under the lights, among the machines, and stood motionless around the narrow tables.

APPLES

George Bowering

In the orchards outside Lawrence the sprinklers are always going, moved twice a day from row to row, & the sun shines every day, so the grass never stops growing. The farmers have to send their mowers down between the trees, cutting the weeds & grass continually. But around each tree where the machine doesn't reach there is a circle of tall grass, sometimes the height of a man, & in this grass the pheasants hide during the day.

Frances Sinclair was walking in her father's small orchard at dusk after supper. With her was a boy from high school who was not George Delsing. George Delsing was the kid from town who was telling her lately that he loved her & she was beginning to believe him. But she had known this other boy for a longer time partly because they both sang in the choir at the Anglican church. Both their fathers had been in the British services during the war, though in different branches.

They were walking in grass that had been cut a few weeks earlier & it was dry because it was two rows away from the sprinkler line. In the approaching darkness they couldn't see the sprinklers but they could hear them clicking in that sound that resembles grasshoppers. It was the beginning of summer so the apples on the trees were small green things & the props hadn't yet been put under the branches though the trees had been thinned and there were many hard green apples on the ground, most of them hidden in the grass.

The boy stopt & held her to him & kisst her with open

lips. She was always impatient with the tight way George Delsing kisst her but these lips were large & soft & she put her arms around his waist as she felt their tongues on one another. They walkt further away from the house with their arms around each other's waists. She could feel his warm hard flesh thru his summer shirt. He played for the volleyball team & he wasn't as graceful as George Delsing but he was stronger. The next time they stopt he put his hand on the front of her shirt as he had done before & she opened her mouth wider.

As they approacht the tall grass under a tree a pheasant crasht up past their faces. It always happened that way. It's a shock because it's so sudden & so loud. Her heart was thumping so that it pickt up the sound of the bird's wings as it disappeared in the dim light. The boy took advantage of this & brought her down gently in the grass & held her while he kisst her & put his hand inside her shirt & inside her bra—it had been repaired twice & it broke again as he was trying to undo it with his arm around her & she lifted her leg to put it around his leg but each time she moved she had to stop & reach around behind her & throw away one of the little apples. Her skirt was half undone & then lifted & he had his hand wet on her, his finger in her & she had grass in her face & his breath, who is this she wondered, & he had always wanted to do this, she had seen his erection under the dark cloth in the choirloft, but she had to, sometime, there was no real trouble because the pain was very little but so was the pleasure & it didn't last long & immediately afterward his kisses stopt & he just held her & that was all. With their parents seeing each other all the time they would be seeing each other all the time & they would probably do it again or she would with George Delsing & as in the book it would get better as you went along, in the orchard or in the bedroom under the pointed roof in the attic or in the hills when he or another managed to borrow his father's car. Or here, in her father's orchard, filled with life or pheasants, mice among the empty boxes, & even the skunks you saw from time to time strutting between the trees. The liquid on her skin was suddenly cold now. She reacht down &

pusht her skirt down a little. They hadn't said a word to each other since they left the house. It must have been unnecessary because they were going thru a necessary step in the pattern. Here I lie, Frances Sinclair, no longer maiden. Now she could hear the sprinklers, shik-shik, shik-shik, shik-shik, shik-shik . . . .

It wasn't long before he grunted & began to gather the front of his pants together & she reacht for the broken old thing & reacht to close her shirt. As she did, she saw the eggs. They lay on the broken grass well hidden by the tall stems. Isn't it late for eggs? One was broken & solid inside. The rest were still all right.

But the pheasant won't come back to them now. You are taught not to touch the eggs or the young because the mother will abandon them. She could do something with the unbroken ones. She could take them & put them among the eggs under the brooding hen. But she couldn't do it right now, she'd have to come back later before it got too cold in the night.

She put her old broken bra over a twig as close as possible to the bottom of the tree.

What are you doing that for? he askt.

Kind of a marker, she said.

He smiled in the dark, tucking in his shirt. What are you, proud or sentimental?

I just want to remember, she said.

AMARYLLIS

Marian Engel

He was the cleanest baby they had ever seen, so fastidious that his mother was worried about him. His nanny, however, assured her that he was a bright little fellow; and wasn't it a blessing to have a sweet little boy after all the big lolloping girls.

He wasn't sure why he was obsessed with order: it had something to do, he thought, with the hugeness of everyone around him, which amounted (because he remained undersize until he had chicken pox in his late teens and "shot up") to gross indecency since he viewed his parents and his sisters from low and unflattering angles. What he was sure of was that for him, everything had to be tidy and intact. He knew it annoyed his family, he knew that his mother particularly considered him to be lacking in spirit, and also, from a very early age, that he was himself, complete as an egg, and would always be this way, and annoy them.

They were prosperous; they lived in one of the great solid houses on the mountain of Montreal; there was never any problem with money. When he decided to make his career in the university, where he could order facts as he ordered his life, no-one protested. This wasn't the kind of mind that would bring scope and drive to the family business, it was a fussy mind, it might, even, for all they knew, be the mind of a homosexual. They gave him his choice of the universities. He went to McGill and Harvard and Oxford and was very happy, and obstinately though fastidiously heterosexual.

His trouble with women was, however, that he liked intellectual women, and the intellectual women he ran into were not interested in housekeeping, and he had friends with similar problems. None of them wanted to marry cows who ran splendid establishments but had nothing to say, but the good minds they met refused to deal with cupboards and scrubbing brushes or even servants. Gloomily, and perhaps too earnestly, he tested his women friends and came to the conclusion that the man who said that brainy women don't wash their hair was right.

Thus he was a bachelor of thirty-one, and well established in his field, when he accepted a vacancy in his discipline at McGill and returned to Montreal, not, firmly, to the house on the mountain, but to a modern bachelor apartment which he fitted with books and white blankets, glass and white plastic furniture, white broadloom.

His mother, having fallen into the habit of introducing young people to each other when she was marrying off the girls (she had done this with distinction), immediately arranged a set of dinner parties for him. His work load was heavy, and he would dash home looking (for him) dishevelled and sit grumpily in the grand dining-room beside or across from the candidates she had chosen, who were on the whole ill-formed or ill-informed, for the girls of their set who had wits had gambolled away on their own years ago. Some of them, he knew, were both brainy and neat and he had missed his chance with them.

So for most of his first year at McGill he was unhappy, and he earned the reputation of being not an eligible bachelor, but a crusty one, though his social coinage remained valuable because of his surname. Toward the end of his second term, at an inter-departmental meeting, he ran into a friend of his undergraduate days, a gusty left-wing sociologist called Ziggy Taler, an irrepressibly untidy man, but a brilliant one. He took Ziggy, who was between wives, home for a drink after the meeting.

"Christ, Alex," Ziggy said, looking around the bachelor nest, "you're the same as ever. Everything in rows and all white. Is it a complex?"

"I don't think so. I think I was born this way."

"Marilyn used to say I was an ink-blot sprouting cigar ash. Couldn't stand me." It was an accurate comparison: he sprawled in the armchair with his tie askew and often missed the ashtray.

This was not, however, the kind of disorder that pained Alexander. Things broken and out of their places upset him, and leaky taps and stockings dripping: ash could be vacuumed.

"I hear," said Ziggy, "that the gold rush is coming to an end. Both your mother and Mrs. Challenor have given up the struggle to find you a wife."

"I hope so."

"Working on a new book?"

"I'm doing the index."

"Yourself? Christ, man, what you need is a round little blonde graduate student. Let me know when you want to come up for air and I'll take you around to meet some people. It's time you got out of that goddam Harvard-Oxford-Westmount ghetto."

Ziggy disappeared for the summer. And Alexander flew to London to check references at the British Museum and attend conferences, but in the fall, finding himself at last with free time, he started dropping in at Ziggy's apartment, where he was liable to meet women of all colours, habits and descriptions, most of whom considered him a reactionary because of his family connections (which were not disguised by his surname) and discussed him unflatteringly to his face. One night, among them, he found a gaunt American poetess named Amaryllis.

She was as tall as his sisters, but differently made, a walking skeleton with large joints and a lantern jaw. She had the hollow voice of the buck-teethed, and tight, straggly blonde curls, and a great mat of blonde hair on her arms and legs. Ziggy told him she was mad as a hatter; that she had finished at the university but hadn't been able either to face graduate work or find a job. "She's bright enough," he said, "but undirected. God, can you imagine anyone focussing that and sending it all off in the same direction?"

She talked fast, but the hollow voice seemed to run behind the mouthing and the gestures, to come from a speaker somewhere else. She seemed by turns naive and supremely wise; she had great, haunted china-blue eyes.

The next day he went with some trepidation to buy her book of poems at Heinemann's. As he was picking it out, the bookseller said, "You'll find that the girl is very good, I assure you." This frightened him even more. He saved the book until after dinner (he cooked for himself, and with finesse), and found out that Heinemann was right, and fell in love with Amaryllis.

She was the child of American eccentrics of good family who had chosen, after *Walden*, to live in the country, and off the land. She had had a queer, isolated childhood, backwoods Maine alternating with expensive boarding schools, and still seemed unsure what to do in a city. When he took her to restaurants she spilled her soup or her wine. She got very drunk, very fast. He found himself adoring her words, and entertaining her more and more in his apartment. He then prudently rented a larger one (she was all right if the pieces of furniture were far enough apart, otherwise she knocked over his little Knoll tables and bumped into bric-a-brac). When he found she wasn't actually living anywhere, only with this friend or that, he asked her to live with him, and, at the end of the year, they decided to marry.

His mother, surprisingly, took to her, though she was annoyed when the engagement received large notice in the *New York Times*, for in addition to the sin of being an American, Amaryllis had committed the solecism of being a pedigreed American (the notice was sent to the papers out of some dim memory of her mother's about how things had once been done) with a list of ancestors beside which Alexander's family looked *nouveau riche*, and was.

They were married in the cathedral between Eaton's and Morgan's, Amaryllis wearing her great-grandmother's yellowish lace and satin, which was not too short. Alexander's sisters attended her and Ziggy was best man: there was a six-inch discrepancy in height between the men's and the women's sides at the altar.

For the first year of their marriage, they went about in

a trance. They were both lonely people, and now they were committed to keep each other company. They liked many of the same things. Although Amaryllis didn't entertain—indeed, she neither knew nor cared about entertaining—she was superbly active, she took him out of himself into sections of the city he had never before penetrated. She fitted into every Bohemian and artistic milieu, did surprisingly well with the academics, and exercised her lively mind on films and plays. Her French was good—indeed, she seemed to lose a good deal of her awkwardness when she translated herself into the more feminine language—and she took him to parties where by himself he would simply have been another Westmount bastard. When they were at home alone he did the cooking. He kept his cleaning-woman, and thought that Amaryllis didn't notice when he re-made their bed, to smooth the creases in the sheets, which hurt him.

About the time when he was beginning his first draft of the third book, however, she became pregnant. She was very sick, and after that, very sleepy. She spent all day in bed surrounded by kleenex and newspapers and basins and trays and couldn't be shunted into the winter cold. His mother and his nanny came to visit her, and, nodding wisely to each other, began to buy for the baby. Amaryllis read Dr. Spock in bed and asked him to make love whenever he passed the bedroom door. She phoned a department store and ordered nursery furniture, then discovered belatedly that they would need a bedroom for it. They moved.

The baby was born in the spring. She called him Tod. Alexander, irritably hoping to be able to spend the summer on his book, noticed that though she spent all her time with him, she rarely changed him. He was, furthermore, although a well-dispositioned baby, inclined to projectile vomiting. The house, which neither of them took much interest in, began to smell.

When he suggested that his elderly nanny come to help, she was angry, and he discovered that she held firm and clear ideas on the subject of child-raising. Tod was not, she insisted, to be turned into a fussy child. Everything was to be nerveless and casual, the child was not to be

107

sacrificed to the furniture or the upholstery; if there were sacred objects he should move them to his study upstairs.

Amaryllis-mother was not the same person as Amaryllis-poet. He consoled himself that most men make the same discovery about their wives; he was involved in an extreme situation because he had married an extreme woman. His work load, however, increased the next year, and it was disheartening to come home to no supper. She learned to scramble a decent egg for Tod, and often made the same effort for him, but the sight of Amaryllis with a paring-knife was unbearable, for she was as unco-ordinated as ever. She could barely change Tod without swallowing his pins, so that he went on having to do the cooking, and since the cleaning-woman had left, the vacuuming (Amaryllis and the machine together suffered from a plethora of elbows), and he phoned the baby-sitters as well because she hated to leave Tod. By the end of the year he was fed to the teeth with marriage.

Tod was a beautiful child, with his mother's fair curls and his father's neat limbs; but he was also a child: he cut up a paper Alex was preparing for the Learned Societies, he rose early and poured ink on the white rugs. Amaryllis began to look guiltily at Alex. Alex began to glower.

"Why don't you write poetry any more?" he asked.

She didn't know, she said. It had something to do with freedom. You wrote poetry, if you wanted to write good poetry, when your mind was free, and she didn't feel free any more. But she warned him not to take it out on Tod.

They went north with a tent that summer. It rained all the time. Amaryllis began to have fits of crying.

When they returned to Montreal, she went on crying—everything seemed to be beyond her. "You should try not to," he said. "It frightens the child."

"The child, is that all he is to you?"

"Tod, then."

"You never make love to me any more."

"You're always asleep or accursed."

She began to cry again.

"You ought to see a psychiatrist."

Then she exploded. "Is that what you think, Alex? Do you think I'm crazy because I'm unhappy with you?

Is that your solution? Neither Toddy nor I have been able to put a foot right for a year. Whenever you look at us a martyred smile crosses your face. We're your cross to bear. You don't even speak to us, you just go around tidying up after us. Why don't you admit you can't stand us?"

He could make no such admission. He did love them, but in such an environment—in the mess, in the stifling hurly-burly of their childishness—he could express nothing.

A week later she took Tod to visit friends in Toronto. She never came back. Alex sold the house and moved his tattered goods to an apartment.

He made vagrant efforts to stay in touch with them, sent them money, sent friends to see that Toddy was well taken care of, sent her a new book he thought she would like. Legally, he supposed, he might have assured the return of the child, but he couldn't part them. He went on with his work, feeling empty and failed, and taught in a small mumbling voice, and was neater and neater.

Amaryllis wrote him several long letters saying she still loved him, explaining the basic disjuncture of their souls, saying Toddy missed him. After a while he heard that she had gone to live with another poet in the country. When she asked for a divorce, he made it easy for her, and, as she had asked, put away money for Tod's education.

Ziggy Taler was disgusted with him. "You let a good girl go without even putting up a fight."

"I suppose I don't like fighting."

"I know, it's not neat. You're turning into an old woman."

"Perhaps I always was one."

When the Separatist movement began to make itself seriously felt, he left Montreal. He belonged by birth to the other camp but Amaryllis and her friends had destroyed his loyalty to it. He didn't feel that there was a place for him in the city.

He went south, across the border, and taught at a midwestern university. The change invigorated him. He began to get his confidence back. His new book on inter-national relations made him a minor celebrity.

When he was offered a job in Toronto, Toddy was eight years old. Alex found that Amaryllis was still living in the country, and had put out two books that he hadn't seen. He accepted the position.

Soon after he settled in Toronto, he met a girl very like himself, admirably suited to him: clever, neat, quiet, serious. She knew Amaryllis, she had in fact edited her poems. She agreed to marry him, but didn't wish to have children, for her career was well established, but not amenable to long interruptions. She thought, however, that it might be good for Tod to come and visit them in the school holidays.

Except for a blank meeting over the divorce, when they hadn't been themselves but dry *papier-mâchè* lawyers' puppets, he hadn't seen Amaryllis for over six years. He drove north to visit her now, following a map she had sent with a cordial invitation.

They were living on the stoney scrublands south of Algonquin Park, along a dirt road that seemed miles from anywhere. Her map was inaccurate, but the village post office knew them well, and directed him. It was afternoon when he drove up their corduroy lane.

Tod, a thin, brown lad with his own face, stopped him half way. "She's chopping wood, mister," he said. "We don't interrupt her." Axe blows fell far apart in the distance, ringing in the clear country air. "Are you Alex?" the child asked. He nodded, and Tod took his hand.

They walked up to the house—a cottage with unpainted board-and-batten siding—when the sound of the axe had stopped. Amaryllis came out beaming, carrying a baby.

He saw her with an awful surge of devotion. Living so much outdoors had consolidated her, she was brown and fat, her faded print blouse was pushed out at the buttons. "Well, Alex, this is Sabina." The baby was fat, too, and ruddy, far different from the waxy infant Tod. He smiled weakly at her.

"Bill's in the woodlot—Tod, run and get him. We're getting the wood in for the winter."

He looked around him and for the first time noticed the blazing autumn colour.

110

"Come in, I'll make you some tea."

The main room of the house contained a woodstove, a crib, and a big pine table surrounded by ladder-back chairs. One end held a collection of instant-coffee bottles. "I'm putting up jam," she said. Then, "I like it here. It's the way I was brought up, you know. I'm sorry I couldn't manage in the city."

"I'm sorry I couldn't either."

"I hear you're marrying Sue. She's exactly right for you."

He was too unhappy to answer.

"We make wine, too. Here, this is Bill's elderberry." It tasted like cough medicine, but it cheered him, or at least cleared his throat so that he could speak again. But as he opened his mouth there was a commotion in the lane.

"Oh Lord, it's the CBC, they're filming us to-day. Who'll I say you are? She handed him Sabina, who began to cry, and then barfed on his shoulder.

Tod and Bill—a bear of a man with a black beard got up to look like a voyageur—came pelting out of the bush. Tod took the baby from him, Bill pumped his hand. "I hear you want young Tod for the holidays."

"If he wants to come."

Amaryllis called out, "Alex, is the cabin tidy?" and dashed in through the screen door. "Oh hell, it looks like us, anyway. They can come in." Alex made his excuses.

"It's the worst possible day," she said. "Come again, will you?"

He made his way back to his car.

Tod came at Easter, since they had agreed by letter that the roads would be too difficult at Christmas, and quietly submitted to expeditions to the Museum and the theatre. But at night he sobbed in his sleep and called out for Amaryllis and Sabina.

On the fourth day, Alex asked him gently if he would like to go home. He said "Yes, please," avoiding his father's eye. He packed his own suitcase in the neatest possible manner.

Alex left him at the bottom of the frozen lane, and thought that he wouldn't see him again until he was embarking for some foreign war.

WHERE IS THE VOICE COMING FROM?

Rudy Wiebe

The problem is to make the story.

One difficulty of this making has been excellently stated by Teilhard de Chardin: "We are continually inclined to isolate ourselves from the things and events which surround us . . . as though we were spectators, not elements, in what goes on." Arnold Toynbee does venture, "For all that we know, Reality is the undifferentiated unity of the mystical experience," but that need not here be considered. This story ended long ago; it is one of finite acts, of orders, of elemental feelings and reactions, of clear legal restrictions and requirements.

Presumably all the parts of the story are themselves available. The difficulty is that they are, as always, available only in bits and pieces. Though the acts themselves seem quite clear, some written reports of the acts contradict each other. As if these acts were, at one time, too well known; as if the original nodule of each particular fact had somehow received non-factual accretions; or even more, as if, since the basic facts were so clear perhaps there was a larger number of facts than any one reporter, or several, or even any reporter had ever attempted to record. Of facts that are still simply told by this mouth to that ear, of course, even less can be expected.

An affair seventy-five years old should acquire some of the shiny transparency of an old man's skin. It should.

Sometimes it would seem that it would be enough—perhaps more than enough—to hear the names only. The grandfather One Arrow; the mother Spotted Calf; the father Sounding Sky; the wife (wives rather, but only one of them seems to have had a name, though their fathers are Napaise, Kapahoo, Old Dust, The Rump)—the one wife named, of all things, Pale Face; the cousin Going-Up-To-Sky; the brother-in-law (again, of all things) Dublin. The names of the police sound very much alike; they all begin with Constable or Corporal or Sergeant, but here and there an Inspector, then a Superintendent and eventually all the resonance of an Assistant Commissioner echoes down. More. Herself: Victoria, by the Grace of God QUEEN, Defender of the Faith; and witness "Our Right Trusty and Right Well-Beloved Cousin and Councillor the Right Honourable Sir John Campbell Hamilton-Gordon, Earl of Aberdeen; Viscount Formartine, Baron Haddo, Methlic, Tarves and Kellie, in the Peerage of Scotland; Viscount Gordon of Aberdeen, County of Aberdeen, in the Peerage of the United Kingdom; Baronet of Nova Scotia, Knight Grand Cross of Our Most Distinguished Order of Saint Michael and Saint George etc. Governor General of Canada." And of course himself: in the award proclamation named "Jean-Baptiste" but otherwise known only as Almighty Voice.

But hearing cannot be enough; not even hearing all the thunder of A Proclamation: "Now Hear Ye that a reward of FIVE HUNDRED DOLLARS will be paid to any person or persons who will give such information as will lead . . . this Twentieth day of April, in the year of Our Lord one thousand eight hundred and ninety-six, and the Fifty-ninth year of Our Reign . . . . "

Such hearing cannot be enough. The first item to be seen is the piece of white bone. It is almost triangular, slightly convex—concave actually as it is positioned at this moment with its corners slightly raised—graduating from perhaps a strong eighth to a weak quarter of an inch in thickness, its scattered pore structure varying between larger and smaller on its perhaps polished, certainly shiny surface. Precision is difficult since the glass showcase is at least thirteen inches deep and therefore an eye cannot be brought as close as the minute inspection of such a small, though certainly quite adequate, sample of skull would normally require. Also, because of the position

113

it cannot be determined whether the several hairs, well over a foot long, are still in some manner attached or not.

The seven-pound cannon can be seen standing almost shyly between the showcase and the interior wall. Officially it is known as a gun, not a cannon, and clearly its bore isn't large enough to admit a large man's fist. Even if it can be believed that this gun was used in the 1885 Rebellion and that on the evening of Saturday, May 29, 1897 (while the nine-pounder, now unidentified, was in the process of arriving with the police on the special train from Regina), seven shells (all that were available in Prince Albert at that time) from it were sent shrieking into the poplar bluff as night fell, clearly such shelling could not and would not disembowel the whole earth. Its carriage is now nicely lacquered, the perhaps oak spokes of its little wheels (scarcely higher than a knee) have been recently scraped, puttied and varnished; the brilliant burnish of its brass breeching testifies with what meticulous care charmen and women have used nationally advertised cleaners and restorers.

Though it can also be seen, the most cursory glance reveals that the same concern has not been expended on the one (of two) 44-calibre 1866 model Winchesters apparently found at the last in the pit with Almighty Voice. It also is preserved in a glass case; the number 1536735 is still, though barely, distinguishable on the brass cartridge section just below the brass saddle ring. However, perhaps because the case was imperfectly sealed at one time (though well enough sealed not to warrant being disturbed now), or because of simple neglect, the rifle is obviously spotted here and there with blotches of rust and the brass itself reveals discolourations almost like mildew. The rifle bore, the three long strands of hair themselves, actually bristle with clots of dust. It may be that this museum cannot afford to be as concerned as the other; conversely, the disfiguration may be something inherent in the items themselves.

The small building which was the police guardroom at Duck Lake, Saskatchewan Territory, in 1895 may also be seen. It has subsequently been moved from its original place and used to house small animals, chickens perhaps, or pigs—such as a woman might be expected to have to look after. It is, of course, now perfectly empty and clean so that the public may enter with no more discomfort than a bend under the doorway and a heavy encounter with disinfectant. The door-jamb has obviously been replaced; the bar network at one window is, however, said to be original; smooth still, very smooth. The logs inside have been smeared again and again with whitewash, perhaps paint. Within the small rectangular box of these logs not a sound can be heard from the streets of the, probably dead, town.

> Hey Injun you'll get hung for stealing that steer
> Hey Injun for killing that government cow you'll
>   get three weeks on the woodpile Hey Injun

The place named Kinistino has disappeared from the map but the Minnechinass Hills have not. Whether they have ever been on a map is doubtful but they will, of course, not disappear from the landscape as long as the grass grows and the rivers run. Contrary to general report and belief, the Canadian prairies are rarely, if ever, flat and the Minnechinass (spelled five different ways and translated sometimes as "The Outside Hill," sometimes as "Beautiful Bare Hills") are unlike any other of the numberless hills that everywhere block out the prairie horizon. They are not bare; poplars lie tattered along their tops, almost black against the straw-pale grass and sharp green against the grey soil of the plowing laid in half-mile rectangular blocks upon their western slopes. Poles holding various wires stick out of the fields, back down the bend of the valley; what was once a farmhouse is weathering into the cultivated earth. The poplar bluff where Almighty Voice made his stand has, of course, disappeared.

The policemen he shot and killed (not the ones he wounded, of course) are easily located. Six miles east, thirty-nine miles north in Prince Albert, the English Cemetery. Sergeant Colin Campbell Colebrook, North West Mounted Police Registration Number 605, presumably lies under a gravestone there. His name is seventeenth in a very long list of "non-commissioned officers and men who have died in the service since the inception of the force." The date is October 29, 1895, and the cause of death is anonymous: "Shot by escaping Indian prisoner near Prince Albert." At the foot of this grave are two others: Constable John R. Kerr, No. 3040, and Corporal C.H.S. Hockin, No. 3106. Their cause of death on May 28, 1897 is even more anonymous, but the place is relatively precise: "Shot by Indians at Min-etch-inass Hills, Prince Albert District."

The gravestone, if he has one, of the fourth man Almighty Voice killed is more difficult to locate. Mr. Ernest Grundy, postmaster at Duck Lake in 1897, apparently shut his window on the afternoon of Friday, May 28, armed himself, rode east twenty miles, participated in the second charge into the bluff at about 6.30 PM, and on the third sweep was shot dead at the edge of the pit. It would seem that he thereby contributed substantially not only to the Indians' bullet supply, but his clothing warmed them as well.

The burial place of Dublin and Going-Up-To-Sky is unknown, as is the grave of Almighty Voice. It is said that a Metis named Henry Smith lifted the latter's body from the pit in the bluff and gave it to Spotted Calf. The place of burial is not, of course, of ultimate significance. A gravestone is always less evidence than a triangular piece of skull, provided it is large enough.

Whatever further evidence there is to be gathered may rest on pictures. There are, presumably, innumerable pictures of the policemen in the case, but the only one of importance is of Sergeant Colebrook, who apparently insisted on advancing to complete an arrest after being warned three times that if he took another step he would be shot. The picture must have been taken before he joined the force; it reveals him as a large-eared young man, hair brush-cut and ascot tie, his eyelids slightly drooping, almost hooded under thick brows. Unfortunately a picture of Constable R.C. Dickson, into whose charge Almighty Voice was apparently committed in that guardroom and who after Colebrook's death was convicted of negligence, sentenced to two months' hard labour and discharged, doesn't seem to be available.

116

There are no pictures to be found of either Dublin (killed early by rifle fire) or Going-Up-To-Sky (killed in the pit), the two teenage boys who gave their ultimate fealty to Almighty Voice. There is, however, one said to be of Almighty Voice, Junior. He may have been born to Pale Face during the year, two hundred and twenty-one days that his father was a fugitive. In the picture he is kneeling before what could be a tent, he wears striped denim overalls and displays twin babies whose sex cannot be determined from the double-laced dark bonnets they wear. In the supposed picture of Spotted Calf and Sounding Sky, Sounding Sky stands slightly before his wife; he wears a white shirt and a striped blanket folded over his left shoulder in such a manner that the arm in which he cradles a long rifle cannot be seen. His head is thrown back; the rim of his hat appears as a black half-moon above eyes that are pressed shut in, as it were, profound concentration; above a mouth clenched thin in a downward curve. Spotted Calf wears a long dress, a sweater that could also be a man's dress coat, and a large fringed and embroidered shawl that would appear distinctly Doukhobour in origin if the scroll patterns on it were more irregular. Her head is small and turned slightly toward her husband so as to reveal her right ear. There is what can only be called a quizzical expression on her crumpled face; it may be she doesn't understand what is happening and would have asked a question, perhaps of her husband, perhaps of the photographer, perhaps even of anyone, anywhere in the world if such questioning were possible for an Indian woman.

There is one final picture. That is one of Almighty Voice himself. At least it purports to be of Almighty Voice himself. In the Royal Canadian Mounted Police Museum on the Barracks Grounds just off Dewdney Avenue in Regina, Saskatchewan it lies in the same showcase, as a matter of fact immediately beside, that triangular piece of skull. Both are clearly labelled, and it must be assumed that a police force with a world-wide reputation would not label such evidence incorrectly. But here there is an ultimate problem in making the story.

There are two official descriptions of Almighty Voice.

117

The first reads: "Height about five feet, ten inches, slight build, rather good looking, a sharp hooked nose with a remarkably flat point. Has a bullet scar on the left side of his face about 1 1/2 inches long running from near corner of mouth towards ear. The scar cannot be noticed when his face is painted but otherwise is plain. Skin fair for an Indian." The second description is on the Award Proclamation: "About twenty-two years old, five feet, ten inches in height, weight about eleven stone, slightly erect, neat small feet and hands; complexion inclined to be fair, wavy dark hair to shoulders, large dark eyes, broad forehead, sharp features and parrot nose with flat tip, scar on left cheek running from mouth towards ear, feminine appearance."

So run the descriptions that were, presumably, to identify a well-known fugitive in so precise a manner that an informant could collect five hundred dollars—a considerable sum when a police constable earned between one and two dollars a day. The nexus of the problem appears when these supposedly official descriptions are compared with the supposedly official picture. The man in the picture is standing on a small rug. The fingers of his left hand touch a curved Victorian settee, behind him a photographer's backdrop of scrolled patterns merges into vaguely paradisiac trees and perhaps a sky. The moccasins he wears make it impossible to deduce whether his feet are "neat small." He may be five feet, ten inches tall, may weigh eleven stone, he certainly is "rather good looking" and, though it is a front view, it may be that the point of his long and flaring nose could be called "remarkably flat." The photograph is slightly over-illuminated and so the unpainted complexion could be said to be "inclined to be fair"; however, nothing can be seen of a scar, the hair is not wavy and shoulder-length but hangs almost to the waist in two thick straight braids worked through with beads, fur, ribbons and cords. The right hand that holds the corner of the blanket-like coat in position is large and, even in the high illumination, heavily veined. The neck is concealed under coiled beads and the forehead seems more low than "broad."

Perhaps, somehow, these picture details could be

reconciled with the official description if the face as a whole were not so devastating.

On a cloth-backed sheet two feet by two and one-half feet in size, under the Great Seal of the Lion and the Unicorn, dignified by the names of the Deputy of the Minister of Justice, the Secretary of State, the Queen herself and all the heaped detail of her "Right Trusty and Right Well-Beloved Cousin," this description concludes: "feminine appearance." But the picture: any face of history, any believed face that the world acknowledges as *man*—Socrates, Jesus, Attila, Genghis Khan, Mahatma Gandhi, Joseph Stalin—no believed face is more *man* than this face. The mouth, the nose, the clenched brows, the eyes—the eyes are large, yes, and dark, but even in this watered-down reproduction of unending reproductions of that original, a steady look into those eyes cannot be endured. It is a face like an axe.

It is now evident that the statement quoted at the beginning has relevance only as it proves itself inadequate to explain what has happened. At the same time, the inadequacy of Aristotle's much more famous statement becomes evident: "The true difference [between the historian and the poet] is that one relates what *has* happened, the other what *may* happen." These statements cannot explain the storyteller's work since, despite the most rigid application of impersonal standards of investigation, the elements of the story have now run me aground. If ever I could, I can no longer pretend to objective, omnipotent disinterestedness. I am no longer a *spectator* of what *has* happened or what *may* happen: I am become an *element* in what is happening at this very moment.

For it is, of course, I myself who cannot endure the shadows on that paper that are those eyes. It is I who stand beside this broken veranda post where two corner shingles have been torn away, where barbed wire tangles the dead weeds on the edge of this field. The bluff that sheltered Almighty Voice and his two friends has not disappeared from the slope of the Minnechinass, any more than the sound of Constable Dickson's voice in that guardhouse is silent. The sound of his speaking is there

119

even if it has never been recorded in an official report:

> Hey Injun you'll get
> hung
> for stealing that steer
> Hey Injun for killing that government
> cow you'll get three
> weeks on the woodpile Hey Injun

The unknown contradictory words about an unprovable act that move a boy to defiance, an implacable Cree warrior long after the three-hundred-and-fifty-year war is ended, a war already lost the day the Cree watch Cartier hoist his gun ashore at Hochelaga and they begin the retreat west; these words are there to be heard just as the unmoving tableau of the three-day siege is there to be seen on the slopes of the Minnechinass. Sounding Sky is somewhere not there, under arrest, but Spotted Calf stands on a shoulder of the Hills a little to the left, her arms upraised to the setting sun. Her mouth is open. A horse rears, riderless, above the scrub willow at the edge of the bluff, smoke puffs, screams tangle in rifle barrage, there are wounds, somewhere. The bluff is green this spring, it will not burn and the ragged line of seven police and two civilians is staggering through, faces twisted in rage, terror, and rifles sputter. Nothing moves. There is no sound of frogs in the night; twenty-seven policemen and five civilians stand in a cordon at thirty-yard intervals and a body also lies in the shelter of a gully. Only a voice rises from the bluff:

> We have fought well
> You have died like braves
> I have worked hard and am hungry
> Give me food

But nothing moves. The bluff lies, a bright green island on the grassy slope surrounded by men hunched forward rigid over their long rifles, men clumped out of rifle-range, thirty-five men dressed as for fall hunting on a sharp spring day, a small gun positioned on a ridge above. A crow is falling out of the sky into the bluff, its feathers sprayed as by an explosion. The first gun and the second

120

gun are in position, the beginning and end of the bristling surround of thirty-five Prince Albert Volunteers, thirteen civilians and fifty-six policemen in position relative to the bluff and relative to the unnumbered whites astride their horses, standing in their carts, staring and pointing across the valley, in position relative to the bluff and the unnumbered Indians squatting silent along the higher ridges of the Hills, motionless mounds, faceless against the Sunday morning sunlight edging between and over them down along the tree tips, down into the shadows of the bluff. Nothing moves. Beside the second gun the red-coated officer has flung a handful of grass into the motionless air, almost to the rim of the red sun.

And there is a voice. It is an incredible voice that rises from among the young poplars ripped of their spring bark, from among the dead somewhere lying there, out of the arm-deep pit shorter than a man; a voice rises over the exploding smoke and thunder of guns that reel back in their positions, worked over, serviced by the grimed motionless men in bright coats and glinting buttons, a voice so high and clear, so unbelievably high and strong in its unending wordless cry.

The voice of "Gitchie-Manitou Wayo"—interpreted as "voice of the Great Spirit"—that is, Almighty Voice. His death chant no less incredible in its beauty than in its incomprehensible happiness.

I say "wordless cry" because that is the way it sounds to me. I could be more accurate if I had a reliable interpreter who would make a reliable interpretation. For I do not, of course, understand the Cree myself.

THE COMING OF AGE

Alden Nowlan

The train had been like every other: the passengers included a soldier, a pair of nuns, a drunken man and a crying baby. The soldier slept, rising and falling in his sleep as a man on horseback rises and falls in the saddle; the nuns, Sisters of Charity, both of whom wore rimless glasses, sat segregated in their black robes as by a screen; the drunken man talked very loudly to his seatmate, a farmer in dairyman's overalls, telling him about the double-header between the Boston Red Sox and the Baltimore Orioles he'd attended the previous weekend— it had been Old Timers' Day in Fenway Park, and Jimmy Foxx, the old double x, had been there, and Dom Dimaggio, the little professor, and Lefty Grove; the baby simply howled until its howl was like a live thing, a bird flying back and forth above the heads of the other passengers, and from time to time its mother got up and walked with it in the aisle, swaying, her face half-hidden by the howling blue blanket-wrapped bundle, patting it and murmuring, "There, there now, there, there."

Kevin had bought two chokingly dry ham and cheese sandwiches, two Cokes and two Crispy Crunch chocolate bars, and they'd eaten and drunk, he and Laura, while the landscape flashed past: telegraph poles, zig-zagging pole fences, moist-looking meadows, grazing cattle, brooks, grey barns, white houses and, once in a while, on the left, a sliver of sea. They hadn't talked much, had said nothing that two strangers thrown together by chance mightn't have said. The strangeness of their situation made him more than normally shy; once when the train rounded a curve she was thrown against him, and he said, "Excuse me; I'm sorry," and then felt ridiculous.

At Tarleton Junction they learned there would be no train leaving for Boston until the following morning. So they walked, carrying their bags, her black cardboard suitcase and his duffle bag, to what appeared to be the town's only hotel. It was a fairly long walk and Kevin imagined that many of the people they passed on the street blinked at them inquisitively. We must look like a couple of God-damn hicks, he thought, wishing he'd had sufficient sense to hire one of the cabs that had been parked at the end of the station platform. He was also ashamed that at the station lunch counter he'd said, "no sugar, please," to the waitress from whom they'd ordered coffee when, of course, the sugar was there, almost in front of him, in a little dish with a kind of spout, and the waitress had nothing whatever to do with it. "That guy said he didn't want sugar," he overheard her telling the short-order cook. "So what," the cook snapped. "Maybe he don't like sugar." But he replied in that manner, Kevin knew, only because he was overworked and annoyed with the waitress for having the time to tell such little jokes. The worst of it was that Kevin was aware that the waitress was amused not so much by his ignorance as by his red-faced and, for an instant, almost wild-eyed embarrassment.

When at length they found themselves alone in the room with the coin-operated radio, the bed tables scarred by cigarette burns and the framed photogravure prints of Banff National Park, the Halifax citadel and a team of oxen standing under an apple tree in blossom, he felt an almost intoxicating sense of relief; it was as if they'd reached a sanctuary. "I wish we could stay here for ever and never go out," he said, seating himself on one of the twin beds and leaning back with his arms behind his head so that he was half sitting and half lying down.

"God, you do have some morbid thoughts," Laura said. She was undressing. "The first thing I'm going to do is take a long hot bath. I'm going to soak until my skin wrinkles. That train was like a pig pen. I feel greasy all over." He shifted his eyes as she slipped out of her

123

underpants. "Oh, darling, you are funny," she said.˚Her voice was amused, but tender. He could hear her smiling.

"Bitch," he said, reaching out for her.

"Not now," she said, pulling away. "Later." She went into the bathroom, naked except for her sandals. Moments later he heard her urinating. He winced. Why hadn't she shut the door? Then he was angry at himself for being so fastidious, another Jonathan Swift. Still, weren't women supposed to have a greater sense of delicacy? He heard her flush the toilet and turn on the tub. "Balls," she said, "the damn water's the colour of mud."

They had met six months earlier. "Somebody's movin' onto the old Pratt place," Kevin's father had said. "You best take a hike over there and see if you can give them a lift." So Kevin had got on his bicycle and ridden down the road to the old Pratt place, which to a stranger would have looked no different from a dozen other farms in the settlement. This was thin-soil country and many of the farms were no longer worked. The Pratt place was a white-washed wood frame house with lightning rods on its roof; an unmown yard; a swaybacked barn topped by a weathervane carved in the shape of a rooster; apple trees, rose bushes and a rhubarb patch, all of them running wild; and a rusted horse rake abandoned in a field.

There had been nothing much for Kevin to do there. In such a situation there was no-one to give orders, and he was too shy to volunteer, so he either stood out of the way, feeling stupid and superfluous, or struggled to find room to take hold of a stove or a sofa that was already in motion, with more than enough men to carry it. How he envied the men who devised ingenious methods of putting long-legged tables through narrow doorways or found the rollers and burlap needed to move a stove without scratching a hardwood floor!

"You look the way I feel," Laura had said. Her long black hair was tied up in a pirate-chief kind of kerchief. She wore a red blouse, its tails knotted at her waist, and tight blue jeans streaked with dust. She was laughing at him, and being laughed at usually filled him with a rage that was almost epileptic in its intensity. But this time it was different: he laughed with her.

"I live up the road a ways," he said. "My name's Kevin O'Brien. Most people call me Kev."

"Hello, Mr. Kevin O'Brien," she said. He glanced down at her feet, which were bare; there were bits of pink polish on her toenails. "I know," she laughed. "I look godawful."

"What? No, that wasn't what I was thinking. You look great."

"You're sweet," she said. "You're a terrible liar, but you're sweet. I'm Laura. We're going to live here in Dracula's Castle. That's my lord and master standing over there between the three-legged table and the easy chair that looks as if it were moulting."

He had already met Peter Trenholm. "How are you doin', kid," the man had said. He had red hair and his arms were so freckled that the skin was almost solidly orange.

"Let's go some place where we can take a load off our feet," she said. "They'll never miss us."

Obediently he followed her around the house, away from the others. They sat down on the back step and looked out over the fields, toward the woods. The sounds of men talking and moving furniture about seemed to come from very far away. "God," she said, "it's so desolate. The grass. And that wind. How do people keep from going crazy?"

"Some of them don't," he said. "No, it's not all that bad. Not really. Not when you get used to it." He wondered what she'd say if he told her he thought it beautiful.

Several weeks later he had admitted it. And she merely smiled. "How many other places have you been?" she said.

"I've never been anywhere," he said, bitterly, as though confessing to a weakness for which there was no hope of remedy.

"Poor old Kevin. Don't take it so hard. You've got all the time in the world. You're just a kid."

"I'm not a kid," he said. "I'm nineteen."

"Liar," she said.

"I was eighteen in January."

By then he was showing her his watercolours and talking to her about the books he borrowed each Saturday from the regional library in Windsor. "Listen to this, Laura," he would say. " 'Your joy is your sorrow unmasked. And the selfsame well from which your laughter rises is oftentimes filled with your tears.' That's from *The Prophet*. By Kahlil Gibran. He came from Lebanon. Isn't it great?"

He tried to teach her to play chess, and she tried to teach him to play the guitar. They went bicycling together, like children, riding across the abandoned airport that had been an RCAF training school during the war, and picnicking in the grass at the end of the runways.

They listened to her collection of records. His favourites were Nat King Cole singing *Lavender Green*, and Fats Domino singing *Blueberry Hill*. He also liked *The Third Man Theme*.

Peter was an NCO with the permanent militia in Halifax, home only during the weekends.

But his great dream was to be a farmer. A farmer was his own boss, Pete said, and didn't take orders from anybody. On Saturdays and Sundays he worked at repairing the barn; or he thinned carrots he had planted, and which he hoped to sell to a wholesaler in Windsor; or he mended fences, stripping to his army boots and khaki shorts and pounding the posts into the ground with a sledgehammer. He talked of buying hens; there was going to be big money in poultry, he said.

"He's a worker," Kevin's father said, awarding his highest compliment. "But that woman of his—well, it's none of my business."

"Pete doesn't know what it's like for me, being shut up here," Laura said to Kevin one evening as he prepared to go home. "It's like being in prison, in solitary confinement. If it wasn't for you, Kevin, I really would go crazy."

He kissed her. It was a very cautious kiss and in bestowing it he stepped on her foot. "Ouch," she said.

"I'm sorry," he said. "I'm a damn fool; somebody should take me out and shoot me."

"Poor Kevin," she said. "Poor old Kevin." They

were standing in the centre of the living-room. She pressed her mouth hard against his, and kept it there; her hand reached under his shirt and began stroking the small of his back.

He drew back his head a little. "Laura," he said. "Laura, I love you."

She put her index finger on his lips. "Don't be silly," she said. "You don't have to say that."

"But it's true," he said. "I do love you." He laid his hand on her buttocks, half-expecting her to push it away. Instead, she used her free hand to unzipper her jeans. "Put it in," she murmured when he hesitated. "Your hand. Put it into my pants. Now the other side. Farther down. There. That's right. Do you like that?"

"Jesus," he said. "Jesus."

She laughed. "Let go of me a second." Very quickly she took off her blouse, jeans and brassiere. "Damn," she said. "I better lock the door."

To tell the truth he was scared. He almost wished he could go home now and think about what had happened. It was pride rather than desire that prevented him from mumbling stupidly, "It's late; I'd better be going."

"Hurry up," she said to him when she came back.

"What?"

"Hurry up and strip. You want to, don't you?" This was not the way it happened in the sex manuals; there girls were timid and had to be aroused gently.

"Sure," he said. As he unbuttoned his shirt he tried to recall whether his underwear was clean. Then he thought how for as long as he could remember his mother had been telling him never to leave the house in dirty underwear. A person never knew what might happen, she said. He giggled.

Naked, he avoided looking down at himself, and scarcely looked at her. For the moment he was so overcome by the suddenness and strangeness of it that he was almost drained of desire.

"Come here," she said. She kicked off her sandals and stood naked except for her underpants. He went to her. "Now. Take off my panties. No. Slowly. Very slowly. Here. Put your hands there. Both hands. Flat. That's it. Now. Press down. Not so hard. Slowly. That's it. Peel me."

That had been the beginning of the series of events that led to their arrival at this hotel. They were off to Boston with the two hundred and seventeen dollars and fifty cents that Kevin had saved that summer while shovelling gravel for the provincial department of highways.

Off to Boston in the green, in the green. Good old Boston, the home of the bean and the cod. In the Yew-nighted States of Amerikay.

He glanced through a leaflet that had been left on the bedside table. It informed him that Tarleton Junction had been the scene of an 18th-century battle between the British and a party of French and Indians led by Coulon de Villiers, who later defeated George Washington at Fort Necessity. The town was the rubber boot capital and transportation hub of eastern Canada, the leaflet boasted.

"Hungry?" Laura asked when she came out of the bathroom. "I could eat a horse."

"We're getting to be just like two old married people," he said, grinning at her.

"Well, you can't eat the other thing," Laura replied.

By now it was dark. They ate in a Chinese restaurant where the waitress wore bedroom slippers and chewed on a toothpick, causing them to giggle like over-tired children. Laura ordered egg rolls and a steak with soya sauce and green peppers, and Kevin, who had never tasted either dish, said simply: "The same." There was a pinball machine which they played while waiting for their food, and a jukebox on which Eddy Arnold, the Tennessee Plowboy, sang about a roomful of roses. They drank beer until all the hard sharp edges became soft, smooth and round.

"I can just hear the old man," Kevin said, wiping foam from his lips with the back of his hand, "he's saying, I knew it, I knew it all along; I made me a half-wit when I made that one."

"I don't suppose Pete's even noticed that I'm gone," Laura said. "Two or three weeks from now somebody will ask him where his wife is, and he'll look up from whatever it is he's doing, swilling the pig or poisoning the potato bugs, he'll look up from whatever he's doing and say, huh, what's that you said, why, I hadn't noticed, but I guess she is gone, now that you mention it."

She laughed loudly. "People are looking at us," Kevin said.

"Let them look for God's sake. We own as much of the world as they do."

The jukebox was playing "Rambling Rose." Their knees touched under the table. She smelled of the eau de cologne he had bought for her. "Look at the label," he had said. "It's the only real cologne there is. The others are just imitations. This is made in Cologne, the city of Cologne, in Germany."

"It's not too late for you to go back," she said.

"Why the hell would I want to go back?"

"You're just a kid, Kevin. Remember, I'm seven years older than you."

"Six," he said. "Look, do we have to go over all that again? It makes me itch. Tomorrow night this time we'll be in Boston."

"Where the streets are paved with gold," she said. "Poor old Kevin."

He finished his beer. "Let's do something," he said. "Even if we just go to a movie."

"Okay," she said.

Ray Milland and Lana Turner had murdered Lana Turner's husband. Ray Milland had loaded the victim's body into the trunk of his car and was driving into the country, where he intended to abandon it. But he needed transportation back; so Lana Turner was following him in a second car. She had never learned to drive. She didn't even know how to turn on the windshield wipers. It began to rain . . . .

Afterwards they stopped for hamburgers and more beer, and then returned to the hotel.

At one point Kevin said to her: "Did I ever tell you about the weird daydream I used to have about running away?"

"No," she said. "I don't think so." She sounded weary.

"It was like being born all over again," Kevin said.

"I'd leave everything behind, you see. Everything. I'd leave the house late at night, after everybody was asleep—I never really did this but it's what I used to tell myself I was going to do—I'd leave the house after everybody in the village was asleep. Stark naked. The way I came into the world. With nothing. I'd leave my name behind, too. I wouldn't be Kevin O'Brien any more. I even used to wish I could take the fillings out of my teeth and leave them behind me. I'd go somewhere else and be somebody new." He laughed. "I even thought out the details; I was going to climb into a truck while the driver was having lunch—Little Orphan Annie was always doing that, and it always worked for her." He laughed again. "The truck wouldn't stop again until it got to, oh, I don't know, Arizona maybe, or British Columbia, and then I'd get out without being seen, and maybe steal some clothes off a clothesline or break into a clothing store . . . . "

"Poor Kevin," she said.

"I wish you'd stop saying that."

"I'm sorry," she said.

"It's okay. I'm sorry I snapped at you. I'm just tired, I guess."

"It's the beer."

They undressed and made love and almost immediately afterwards he fell asleep.

He dreamt they had missed the train and were running after it, down the tracks, shouting for it to stop. He dreamt they boarded the train and discovered it was not a train but a roller coaster, and the car in which they sat also contained a fully decorated Christmas tree and a coffin.

He was awakened next morning by the sound of distant bells. He had forgotten that today was Sunday. "What time is it?" he said. Then he realized that the other bed was empty.

"Laura?" he called. The bathroom door was open; he got up and looked inside, although it was obvious that no-one was there.

Perhaps she was teasing him. Feeling an utter fool he actually looked under the beds and in the closets.

Her suitcase was gone.

He sat down. Then he got up again and made another search of the room, this time looking for the suitcase. No doubt she had moved it when she dressed. How Laura would laugh at him when he confessed that for a little while he had been afraid that she—. He saw the note lying on the chest of drawers, in front of the mirror.

It was written in pencil on a sheet of paper headed *Royal Hotel, Tarleton Junction, Transportation Hub of Eastern Canada,* and it read:

Kevin I'm sorry Laura.

His mind wouldn't tell his body how to react; so for a long moment he did nothing. Then he laughed.

He laughed again when he found that she had taken five twenty-dollar bills from his pocketbook.

He lay down, buried his face in the pillows and cried a little.

He rolled over on his back, dried his eyes on a corner of a pillowcase, and laughed again.

It didn't occur to him to go out looking for her, although he realized she might still be at the railway station. He lay on the bed all morning, not so much thinking as waiting for some thoughts to come. At noon he discovered to his surprise that he was hungry.

THE LATE MAN

Andreas Schroeder

On the morning after the storm, the fishermen got up earlier than usual to survey the damage and repair what could be saved. Unusually strong winds and rain had scattered the nets and flattened gardens, bushes, even trees. Fishing boats lay strewn about the beach like broken teeth. Everywhere an exhausted silence hung limply; even the occasional seagull screech seemed blunted and uncertain. Across the mud-flats the faint rush of breakers seemed to fade, though the tide was coming in, slowly and without apparent conviction.

At this time in the morning the fishermen rarely spoke. They arranged their lines, oiled pulleys, checked over their engines and wordlessly pushed out to sea. To break the fragile silence of the first few hours would have been like bursting a delicate membrane without preparation; it was tacitly understood that a man needed more time to clear away in his mind the rubble and destruction of the preceding night than was available to him between his getting up and the launching of his boat. Even after they had cleared the beach and set their course for the large fishing-grounds farther north, the fishermen rarely raised their voices—as if in instinctive respect for the precariousness of the human mind launched before sunrise on an uncertain sea.

But someone broke the silence that morning; as the last remaining boats poled into deeper water to lower their engines, a young bearded fisherman pointed to a single unattended boat lying on its side on the beach and asked in a low voice: "Where's he?"

The man being addressed looked startled, puzzled, then shrugged his shoulders.

The bearded fisherman risked a further offence. "Could he be sick, d'you think?"

There was no reponse. The other man slid his oar into the water and pushed them off.

A man opens his cabin door and steps into view. He is the late man, the man whose boat still lies untouched on the beach below his cabin. There is nothing particularly unusual about this man except perhaps a certain slight hesitation in his manner; the hesitation of a man for whom the world became at some point intensely suspect, for whom, at that point, a glass on a table became less and less a glass on a table and more and more a thing too strange and amazing to grasp by name. As he stands in his doorway, his hand rests gingerly on the frame, as if constantly ready in case of attack.

About fifteen minutes have passed since the last boat was launched and the late man stepped from his cabin. Now, his boat ready and his outboard spluttering half-submerged, he pushes off and follows the fleet toward the fishing-grounds.

A few hours later the fishing village begins to yawn, stretch and get up; children and fishwives clutter the streets and tangle the air with punctuation marks.

When they return in the early evening and pull their boats out of the water above the high-tide markers, the late man is not with them. During the interval of time between the last fisherman's ascent from his stranded boat to his waiting dinner and the late man's arrival at the launching site fifteen minutes later, silence holds the beach like an indrawn breath. The sound of his prow on the pebbles, therefore, grates in an unusually harsh way on the nerves of the woman waiting for him above the high-tide markers. He has caught fewer fish than the other fishermen.

The next morning the late man appears at his cabin door half an hour after the fishermen have left the beach.

Their boats are already vague in the distance when he finally manages to haul his boat to the water-line, which has by this time fallen far below his landing place with the receding tide. He seems somehow weakened, older, leaning wearily against the wheel of his boat. When the fishermen return that night he is an uncertain speck on the horizon, half an hour behind the last of the fishing fleet, and when the catch is scored, he has caught fewer fish than the day before.

Around noon the following day the boats were anchored in clusters to share both lunch and small-talk on the fishing-grounds, and the conversation turned to the late man. "Can't figure 'im out," one fisherman mused, pulling thoughtfully at his beard. "Won't tell nobody what's wrong." "Ain't sayin' a thing," another agreed. "Asked him yesterday what the problem was, but I'll be damned if he didn't seem like he wasn't even listening." There was a pause as if to let the spoken words disperse. Then: "Sea can do that to a man. Catches up with him, it does." The speaker slowly shook his head, threw an orange peel overboard, then absently ignored a deck-hand who had asked him what he meant. The deck-hand finally turned away, assuming his question was naive; he was new in the fleet and often found himself being unanswered. As it was, he was already on the other side of the boat when the old man muttered his answer to no-one in particular: "I don't know what happens; I just know it does. Ain't no man can whirl the world by hand."

The next morning the late man launched his boat some forty-five minutes after the fleet had left the beach.

Little is known of the late man's history, though this isn't realized until he first begins to attract attention by his mystifying dislocation of schedule; suddenly everyone rummages about in their memory for initial impressions, former opinions, latent suspicions, old predictions. Little in the way of substantial information is collected. It is generally agreed that he is a relatively young man, hard-working and "well-disciplined." Some feel him to be a little too much given to reflection, but one suspects this is said chiefly in reaction to his if not exactly anti-social, at least fairly reticent manner. He cares little for other people, though he has been known to go to the aid of a complete stranger for no reason. A slightly more observant villager notes his peculiar tendency to touch (with a curiously disbelieving air) whatever happens to be around him; the remark is received in uncertain silence. Many frankly admit they have no idea what to make of the whole business, and that the man is probably simply under the attack of some unsettling virus. This fails to explain, however (as someone quickly points out), his consistent, almost plan-like deceleration of pace in relation to the normal fishing schedule of the village—by this time he is reported leaving the beach a full three hours after the last of the other boats has been launched.

By the time the late man pulls his boat from the water, the sun is little more than an almost-submerged leer on a mindless horizon and the waves have jelled to heavy, slowly swirling jibes. Night winds begin to cover the eastern part of the sky with a thick, cumulous ceiling of ridicule. Sardonic chuckles ripple along the waterline where the undertow pursues an endless foreplay with beach gravel. The late man stands motionless, looking strangely as if he belongs neither to the water nor the land; his face is a ploughed field but his eyes dart about the beach like frightened piranhas. His boat is a crazily tilted sneer lying on its side in the pebbles, with rope dangling from the prow like corded spittle. Wave upon wave of curling laughter lampoons the beach. Everywhere, everything grins. The late man no longer defends himself. He has committed the blunder of allowing himself and the universe to discover his detective activities, his secret investigations into the nature and composition of himself and whatever he finds it possible to apprehend. But he has allowed this discovery prematurely, before he has had time to properly anaesthetize his specimens, and now, suddenly aware of a spy in their midst, they have disintegrated into countless labyrinthine possibilities and traps and the late man is cut off without the possibility of retreat. He has long since given up trying to sledge-hammer his brain to sleep.

But a violated universe will not be satisfied with the simple deflection of an inquisitive mind, and as if to make certain that such a trespassing will never again be possible, it has turned glaring spotlights against the late man's brain, blinding and overwhelming it with confusion and derision. Stiffly aligned principles and corollaries suddenly go limp and begin to collapse; endless qualifications overrun simple premises and leave behind a shambles of tattered and useless shreds of belief. Above all, the horror is set creeping up the back stairs of the late man's mind that all this is beyond his control, and that like a retaining pin pulled from a spring-loaded wheel, this destruction will continue relentlessly until it has unrolled the tension from the spring.

There appears to be little he can do but to hold on until all is done, and to hope that he doesn't become so weakened in the process as to fall prey to a useless madness.

In a matter of months the departures and arrivals of the late man and the fishing fleet have diverged to such an extent that the returning fishermen see the late man's boat heading toward them at dusk, on its way north toward open water. He stands huddled over his wheel, eyes staring unseeing at the darkening horizon as if in purposeful blindness. The fishing fleet parts to let him pass; though no one appears to understand, everyone sees the desperate undertow in his eyes and says nothing. When all the boats are secured and the gear locked away, the late man is a dissolving blotch against black evening. A few moments later he is gone.

The late man had returned the previous morning with no fish at all.

As he sat down to dinner, the young fisherman who had asked about the late man early one morning suddenly spoke of him to his wife. "Nobody knows anything, or they won't say anything. Everybody pretends to ignore him. I've got to find out."

His wife said nothing. He looked at her curiously, then threw down his knife. "Well damn it, here's a man

136

digging his own grave in plain view of a whole village, and nobody has the guts to look into the matter." His wife remained silent but a worried look began to unsettle her face. The young fisherman stood up abruptly. "I'm going to find out." he said, reaching for his squall-jacket and opening the door. "Even if for no other reason than a simple matter of self-defence!" he added as the door slammed shut. Footsteps receded from the cabin. Within minutes the sound of his outboard began to move across the bay toward the fishing grounds and the open sea.

For a time the young fisherman directs his boat through thick total darkness; a bulging cloud-cover muffles the moon and the night sways and sidesteps in ponderous movements that are blind but everywhere. The occasional clear splash falls short among the sluggish gurgle and sagging cough of deep-water waves beneath the keel. The young fisherman peers at the bleakness but steers his boat by instinct.

As he moves farther and farther into deeper water the night begins to thin out; his eyes detect edges, outlines, occasional glimpses of phosphoric glitter—eventually the moon disentangles from the clouds and trudges higher into the sky, spraying a fine shower of thin light over the fishing grounds. By this time the young fisherman can make out the dark shape of the late man's boat, lying at anchor on his starboard side. The young fisherman shuts off his engine and drifts closer. The booms on the boat before him are out, trailing thin glistening lines into the water. The late man is fishing.

The young fisherman sits unmoving at his wheel, uncertain as to what should follow. Possibilities dart in and out of his mind, unwilling to bite. He waits, his brain idling slowly, his thoughts loose.

A creak from a rusty tackle interrupts the silence. A glass float dips and scrambles; the late man comes alive and begins to reel it in. A strike.

The young fisherman straightens up and strains to see. The glass float tugs and splashes at the end of a stiff line; the late man's figure curves against the mast, his arms taut like two rigid claws shaking with exertion. The young fisherman feels an instinctive excitement thrill through his body as if the strike were his own. Something huge is on the end of that line.

The glass float is almost at boat's-edge, momentarily calmer. The late man reaches for his fish-net and plunges it over the side, scooping carefully. His back is turned to the young fisherman, obscuring the float as he brings it to the boat's side. The fish-net rises from the water, then stops.

Surprised, the young fisherman leans forward but sees only the hunched back of the late man leaning over his net. A fierce rippling movement shakes the arm holding the handle as something twists and writhes in the meshes, but the late man makes no move to pull it into the boat. Ten minutes pass; the late man still stands bent over his net, gazing at his catch. The young fisherman is unable to see his face.

Finally, in a slow but deliberate movement, the late man empties his net into the sea and straightens up.

The young fisherman watches, still dumbfounded, as the late man repeats the same procedure moments later when another line snaps alive. This time his demeanour seems to indicate recognition or less interest; a short look suffices to make him empty the net again. After a short pause a third float begins to bob and the late man reels it in. Half an hour later he is still engrossed in the net's contents ignoring all the other lines which are jerking at the boom. Bent over the gunwale, his hair blowing about his head like spray in the wind, the late man stares at his catch in silence, then throws it back into the sea.

As a faint paleness begins to tinge the outermost edges of the dark, the young fisherman stands up stiffly, a nervous flutter in his stomach, strangely excited yet uncertain why. He detects traces of the intoxication of discovery in his feelings, though he has no idea what he has discovered or realized.

Carefully pulling out his oars, he mounts them in the oarlocks and prepares to slip away. By the time the sun appears he will be back in the bay and his cabin. Then there will be time to think.

A small sound from the other boat stops his raised oars

short. The late man has emptied his net and stepped back toward the mast. As he half-turns to re-apply bait to one of the lines the young fisherman catches a glimpse of the late man's face. He almost drops his oars.

The late man's face is totally disfigured. Crumbled skin, twitching lips and bleached white hair, he is suddenly old—an uncertain fool barely able to hold his balance in the rocking boat. The young fisherman is stunned. The late man was of the same generation as the others in the fishing fleet—chronologically about thirty years old. Now he looks three times that age.

But there is no time to lose; the horizon is becoming a thin pencil-line of light across the dark and he will be discovered. Stealthily moving his oars, the young fisherman pulls away toward the south and the fishing village.

As his boat moves into the bay, he sees the first cabin doors opening and fishermen walking down the beach toward their boats. Several of them look up, surprised to see his incoming boat at such an odd time. Obviously his wife has said nothing. He steers toward an unused part of the beach and runs his boat aground.

There, his boat bouncing slightly to the rhythm of his fading wash, he sat on the bow and twisted a piece of rope between his fingers; uncertain, almost nervous, uncertain again. The spreading sun warmed his back as he sat, but his stomach remained cold and unsettled; he felt the desperate urge to run, to commit a violence, tear something to shreds, but somehow he was numbed or simply unable to move. For no apparent reason something seemed to have snapped; his senses coiled and bunched up in twisting knots, thoughts whirled in ever-tightening circles about his head and a steadily mounting pressure threatened to explode inside him like a surfacing deep-water fish.

Then the faint growl from a distant engine punctured the silence and the tension drained away with an almost audible hiss. The young fisherman looked over his shoulder and watched the late man's boat increase toward the bay. Several of the other fishermen paused and shaded their eyes. For a short while everything hung in suspension . . . .

Suddenly the late man's boat is in the bay, its engine silent, drifting toward the beach. As its prow gouges into the sand the late man struggles feebly to climb off the deck onto the gravel, half-falling several times in the process. Then, hoisting the bow rope over his shoulder, he attempts to pull his boat higher up onto the beach.

Later, after the late man had been buried and the fishermen had returned to their boats, the young fisherman was heard to say that in a totally paralyzed landscape, the only moving thing had been the late man trying to beach his boat. They had watched him for an incredibly long time, trying to raise the bow above the gravel, and when he finally collapsed, still no-one had moved. When they eventually began to climb down toward the fallen figure, the landscape seemed to stretch and expand in every direction and they walked for hours before reaching him. They found him lying on his back, his face contorted with a mixture of agony and amazement; it was the oldest face they had ever seen. So they had buried him, quietly and without looking at each other, and the young fisherman had beached the boat. The next morning, due possibly to the tiring events of the preceding night and day, the young fisherman slept a little longer, and eventually launched his boat some fifteen minutes after the last of the fishing boats had cleared the bay.

IN QUEBEC CITY

Norman Levine

In the winter of 1944 when I was twenty and in the RCAF
I was stationed for seven weeks in Quebec City. Fifty
newly-commissioned pilot officers were billeted in an
old building right opposite a cigarette factory. It used to
be a children's school. The wooden steps were wide and
worn in the middle but they rose only a few inches at a
time.

We were sent here to kill time and to learn how to
behave like officers. Some of the earlier Canadian Air
Force officers who were sent to England lacked the social
graces. So they had us play games. We took turns
pretending we were orderly officers, putting men on
charge; being entertainment officers, providing the escort
for a military funeral. We were taught how to use knives
and forks. How to propose a toast. How to eat and drink
properly. To keep fit we were taken on early-morning
route marches. We walked and ran through frozen
side-streets, then across a bridge to Levis. And came back
tired but with rosy cheeks. Evenings and weekends were
free. We would get into taxis and drive to the top to the
restaurants, have a steak and French fries, see a movie.
On Sunday we behaved like tourists. Took pictures of
Champlain, Bishop Laval, the Golden Dog, the Château
Frontenac, the wall around the city, the steps to Lower
Town. There wasn't much else to do.

On the Monday of the second week Gordie Greenway,
who was make-believe orderly officer for the day, came
up to me during lunch.

141

"Someone rang asking for you."

"Who?" I asked. I didn't know anyone in Quebec.

"They didn't give their name," he said and continued his tour of inspection.

Next morning I received this letter.

Quebec, 15 January

Dear Pilot Officer Jimmy Ross,

We would be honoured if you could come to dinner this Friday. It would give me and my wife much pleasure to meet you. If I don't hear from you I'll take it that we'll see you on Friday at 8.

Mendel Rubin

Out of curiosity I decided to go. The taxi driver drove to the most expensive part, just off Grande Allée, and stopped at the base of a horseshoe drive in front of a square stone building with large windows set in the stone.

I rang the bell.

A maid in black and white uniform opened the door. "Come in, sir," she said with a French accent.

I came inside. A short man in a grey suit came quickly up to me, hand outstretched. He wore rimless glasses and had neat waves in his fair hair.

"I'm so glad you could come," he said smiling. "My name is Mendel Rubin. Let me have your coat and hat. You didn't have any trouble getting here?"

"No," I said.

He led me into the living-room. And introduced his wife, Frieda. She was taller than he was, an attractive dark-haired woman. Then their daughter, Constance. She was around 17 or 18, like her mother, but not as pretty.

"It's very nice of you to ask me over," I said.

"Our pleasure," Mendel said. "Now, what will you drink. Gin? Scotch? Sherry?"

"Gin is fine," I said.

He went to a cupboard at the far end of the room.

"Where are you from?" Frieda asked.

"Ottawa."

142

"I've been there a few times," she said. "But I don't know it well. Mendel knows it better."

He came back with drinks on a tray.

"Do you know the Raports?" he asked. "The Coopers? The Sugarmans?"

"I went to school with some of the kids," I said.

"Where do you live?"

"On Chapel Street—in Sandy Hill."

"It's a part of Ottawa I don't know too well," he said. "What does your father do?"

"He's a teacher."

The maid came in to announce that dinner was ready. As we walked toward the dining-room, he said, "Everytime a new draft comes in I find out if there are any Jewish officers. Then we have them up. It's nice to be with your own kind—you can take certain things for granted. Come, sit down here." And he put me in a chair opposite Constance.

While Mendel talked I had a chance to glance around the room. The walls were covered with some kind of creeper. The green leaves, like ivy leaves, clung to the walls on trellis-work and to the frames of oil paintings. The paintings looked amateurish, as if they had been painted by number.

"Do you like the pictures?" Mendel asked. "My wife painted them."

"They're very good," I said.

Mendel did most of the talking during the meal. He said they were a tiny community. They had to get their rye bread, their kosher meat, flown in from Montreal.

"We're so few that the butcher is only a butcher in the back of the shop. In the front he sells antiques."

After the meal we returned to the other room. It was dimly lit. The chandelier looked pretty but didn't give much light and there were small lights underneath more of Frieda's pictures on the walls. The far wall was one large slab of glass. It had now become a mirror. And I could see ourselves in this room, in the dark glass, as something remote.

Mendel went to a cupboard and brought back vodka, brandy, whisky, liqueurs. He gave me a large cigar.

"You know what I feel like after a meal like that? How about we all go to the theatre?"

"But it's half-past nine," Constance said.

"How time goes when you're enjoying yourself," Mendel said. Then glanced at his wrist. "I think we'll still catch it." He walked to the far cupboard and turned on a radio.

A Strauss waltz was being played. It stopped. And a commercial came on. A sepulchral voice boomed *Rubins*. And then *bins . . . bins . . .* echoed down long corridors. Then another voice spoke rapidly in French. And again *Rubins* and the echoing *bins . . . .*

He switched the radio off.

"I have a store in Lower Town. We carry quality goods and some cheap lines. Sometime I'll show you around, Jimmy. But what can we do *now*?"

"Mummy can play the piano," Constance said. "She plays very well."

"I don't," Frieda protested.

"Play us something," Mendel said.

Frieda went to the piano and played *Fur Elise*, some Chopin, while we drank brandy and coffee and smoked cigars.

At eleven he was driving me back to the children's school.

"Do you know the one about the two Anglican ministers?"

"No," I said.

"There were these two Anglican ministers," Mendel said. "One had seven children. The other had none. The one with the seven children asked the other, "How do you do it?"

"I use the safe period," the other minister said.

"What's that?"

"When *you* go out of the house—*I* come in. It's safe then." And Mendel laughed.

"Here's another one. There was this Jewish tailor. He had an audience with the Pope. When he got back to Montreal they asked him—How was the Pope? A nice little man, the Jewish tailor said. 36 chest, 32 waist, 28 inside leg . . . ."

144

"Are you taking Constance out tomorrow night?"
"Yes." I said.

I took her to a movie. We got on fine. On Sunday we went out in the country to ski. We skied for miles. We both seemed to have so much energy. We came to a long hill. I went down first. She followed and fell at the bottom. I picked her up and we kissed.

"My father is worried that I'll be an old maid," she said laughing.

I didn't think he needed to have any worries about that.

"He only lets me go out with Jewish boys."

We kissed again.

"Am I going to have a baby?"

"You don't have babies that way," I said.

"I know. But I have a girlfriend in Montreal. She told me that if you let a boy kiss you like that you can become pregnant."

Though I was being thrown together with Constance (we went out often for meals, saw movies, had romantic night-rides in a sleigh, wrapped in fur skins, behind the swaying rump of a horse) and Mendel took me to several hockey games, it was Frieda who interested me. But so far I hadn't had a chance to be alone with her. If Mendel was there, he didn't let anyone else talk. If Constance was there, I was expected to be with her.

I managed to get away from the children's school early one Wednesday and drove up to the house to find that Mendel and Constance had driven to his branch store in Three Rivers.

"I was just reading," Frieda said when I came into the living-room.

She got me a drink. We stood by the glass wall looking out. It's a nice time, in winter, just before it gets dark. When the snow on the ground has some blue in it, so has the sky. She told me she came from Saint John, New Brunswick. Her father was a doctor. At seventeen her parents sent her to Montreal. "Just the way we worry about Constance." She met Mendel. He was working for his father who founded Rubins Department Store in

Quebec. She was eighteen when they married and Constance came along when she was nineteen.

"After she grew up I found I had nothing to do with my time. And when I tried things—I found that I can't do anything well. That's my trouble."

"You had Constance," I said.

"Anybody can do that," she said contemptuously.

"I tried to paint—I have all these nice pictures in my head—but look how they come out. I tried writing—but it was the same. Sometimes when I'm walking through the streets or in a restaurant I see something. It excites me. But what can I do with it? There's no-one I can even tell it to. I hardly go out of the house now. I feel trapped."

"Can't you leave Quebec City," I said, "for a short—"

"I don't mean by this place," she interrupted. "I mean by life."

This conversation was out of my depth. I didn't know what she wanted. But her presence excited me far more than Constance did.

"I taught myself French," she said, "so I could read Colette in the original. And I have my flowers. Do you like flowers?"

"Yes," I said. "I like the colours."

She led me to her conservatory. It was full of orchids: yellows, purples, oranges, pinks, browns. There were other exotic flowers. I didn't know their names. There were several creepers overhead. And a smell of jasmine from the one in a corner. But it was mostly orchids, and in different stages. Some were only beginning to grow. They seemed to be growing out of stuck-together clusters of grotesque gooseberries. While outside the glass of the conservatory the thick snow had a frozen crust. It glittered underneath the street lights.

She showed me a striped orchid on the table in the hall. Yellow with delicate brown stripes. It was open and curved in such a way that you could see deep inside the flower.

"Do you know how Colette describes an orchid?"

"No," I said.

"Like a female genital organ—I have shocked you," she said with a smile. "I'd be promiscuous if I were a man.

146

I know it. I wouldn't be like my husband. He's so old-fashioned—telling jokes. But I can't do anything like that here. If I step out of line—"

She broke off again. She would talk, follow a thought, then, unable to see it through, break into something else.

"Poor Mendel. He desperately gets in touch with every Jewish officer who comes to Quebec. Throws them together with Constance as much as he can. Then they go overseas. They promise to write. But they never do."

I heard a car drive up. Mendel and Constance came through the door.

"Hello Jimmy," he said. "Boy it's a cold night."

The other officers complained about the deadness of the place. They thought I was lucky. Some met girls through a church dance or YMCA do. A few could speak French. Most tried to pick something up.

Tucker and Fleming got into trouble and were accused of raping a waitress. But nothing came of the charge, except they were confined for three days to a make-believe cell in the children's school.

I tried to get Frieda alone again. The only time I did she was upset. The boiler to the conservatory had broken down.

"You must get a plumber," she appealed to me. "If I can't get a plumber the orchids will die."

I got a taxi into Lower Town. Half an hour later I came back with a French-Canadian plumber.

Our time was up. To see how we finally passed the Air Force organized a ball at the Château Frontenac and all the eligible debutantes from Quebec and district were invited to be escorted by the officers. I took Constance. She looked very nice in a long white gown. We danced, made small talk, ate, passed the carafe of wine around. The dance band played.

> To you he might be just another guy
> To me he means a million other things
> An ordinary fellow with his heart up
>   in the sky
> He wears a pair of silver wings.

147

Air Marshals made speeches calling us "Knights of the Air," "Captains of the Clouds."

At half past two we left the Château Frontenac. In the taxi, driving back, she pressed against my side.

"Don't you love me a bit, Jimmy?" she said softly.

"I'll be gone in a few days," I said.

She took my hand.

"Would you like to come up to my room? You'll have to be very quiet going up the stairs. I'll set the alarm for six—you'll have to be out by then."

I wondered how many times this had happened before.

"Is this the first time?"

"No," she said. "There've been other officers passing through." She squeezed my hand. "I didn't like them as much as you."

"How many others?"

"Four. This will be my fifth time."

She spoke too soon. After we went up the stairs, closed the door of her room, undressed, got into bed, turned out the light, I found I couldn't do a thing. And she didn't know how to help things along.

"Let's have a cigarette," I said, "and relax for a while."

I lit one for her and one for me. We lay on our backs, the cigarette ends glowing in the dark.

I was wondering what to do when I heard a door open. Then footsteps. Someone was walking in the corridor. The footsteps stopped by the door.

"*Con, are you awake?*"

It was Frieda on the other side.

We both stopped breathing.

"*Con—you awake?*"

She was lying beside me, not moving, frightened, breathing deeply and rapidly.

I waited for the steps to go away, the sound of a far door closing. I put out our cigarettes. And took her easily.

"That was the best yet," she said softly. "Goodnight darling. Wake me before you go."

She lay on her side, away from me, asleep. And I lay on my back, wide awake. I listened to the ticking clock, her regular breathing, and thought of Frieda.

Just after five I got out of bed, dressed, disconnected the alarm, straightened the covers on Constance. And went out of the room, down the stairs and out.

It was snowing. Everything was white and quiet. It felt marvellous walking, flakes slant, very fine. I didn't feel at all tired. I heard a church bell strike and somewhere further the sound of a train whistle, the two notes like the bass part of a mouth organ. The light changed to the dull grey of early morning and the darker shapes of a church, a convent, came in and out of the falling snow.

Next day we were confined to barracks and told to pack. That afternoon we boarded a train for Halifax. And at Halifax we walked from the train onto the waiting troop ship. Two weeks later we docked at Liverpool.

Those first few months in England were exciting. I moved around a lot. A week in Bournemouth in the Majestic Hotel. Ten days leave in London. Then a small station, in Scotland, for advanced flying on Ansons. Then operational training near Leamington on Wellingtons. Before I was posted to a Lancaster Squadron in Yorkshire.

Perhaps it was this moving around? Perhaps it was being twenty, away from Canada for the first time, spring, meeting new people, new situations? The uniform was open sesame to all sorts of places. And there were plenty of girls around. I had forgotten about the Rubins except to send them a postcard from London.

In the middle of May I had an air-letter, re-directed twice, from Constance.

Dear Jimmy,

I hope this will reach you soon. Probably you're having all kinds of exciting things happen to you . . . meeting new people . . . doing things . . . and you have long forgotten me and the time we had together. I hope not.

Now my news. We're just getting over winter. It's been a long one, cold and lots of snow. The next lot of officers after you was a complete washout. But the one now has 3 Jewish officers. Shatsky and Dworkin from Montreal. And Lubell from Winnipeg. None of them are as nice as you . . . but I like Shatsky best . . . he's fun.

Don't forget to write when you can and take care. Mummy and Daddy send their regards. We all miss you. Love,

Constance

Two months later I received a carton of Macdonald cigarettes from Mendel. I bet he sent them to all the boys he had up at the house.

When the war was over I went back to Ottawa and to the job I had had in the Government with the construction department. In my absence I was promoted. Now I'm assistant to the Head.

I haven't married. Nor had I been to Quebec City, until this winter when I had to go to New Brunswick to see about a proposed dam the Federal Government was thinking of putting some money in. The plane stopped at Quebec longer than the usual stop to let off and pick up passengers. A blizzard was blowing. Flying was off. A limousine brought us from the snow fields of the airport to the Château Frontenac. We were told the next weather inspection would take place at 3.

I took a taxi to Lower Town. Down St. Jean. Down the slope. Passed the cheap stores, the narrow pokey side streets, horses pulled milk sleighs, the bargain clothes hung out, the drab restaurants. An alligator of schoolgirls went by along the sidewalk with two nuns behind. Even with the snow falling men doffed their hats to priests.

I found Mendel standing in the furniture department. He looked much older and fatter in the face, the skin under the jaw sagged, and the small neat waves of hair were thin and grey.

"Hullo Mendel," I said.

He didn't recognize me.

"I'm Jimmy Ross," I said. "Remember during the war?"

"Of course," he said, becoming animated. "When did you get in?"

"Just now. The plane couldn't go on to Fredericton because of the snowstorm."

"Let's go and have some coffee next door," he said. "It's been snowing like this all morning."

150

We went to the Honey Dew and had coffee. The piped-in music played old tunes. And bundled-up people with faces down went by the plate-glass window.

"I wish Constance were here," he said. "I know she'd be glad to see you."

"How is Constance?"

"She's living in Detroit. Married. He came over from Germany after the war. His name is Freddie. He's an accountant. They're doing well. They have four kids. And she's expecting another. How about you?"

I told him briefly what I had done.

"There were some good times during the war—" he said.

"How is Frieda?"

"She died a year and a half ago. I married again. Why don't you come up to the house and meet Dorothy."

"I'd like to," I said. "But I don't want to miss the plane."

"They won't take off in this weather," he said. "But here I am telling *you* about airplanes."

"That was twenty-two years ago," I said. "I couldn't fly the airplanes today."

We got into his black Cadillac with black leather seats. He drove through all-white streets, the windshield wipers going steadily, to the house.

Dorothy was the same size as Mendel, plump, a widow, very cheerful.

"This is Jimmy Ross," Mendel said. "He was a young Air Force officer here during the war. He used to be much handsomer." He went to the far cupboard to get some drinks.

The oil paintings, the creepers, the flowers, were gone. A rubber plant stood by the plate-glass wall. Its bottom leaves shrivelled and brown.

"Would you like some sponge cake?" Dorothy asked.

"She makes an excellent sponge," Mendel assured me.

"I had lunch on the plane," I said. "I can't stay very long."

It had almost stopped snowing. Only the wind, in gusts, blew the loose snow up from the ground and down from the roofs.

151

"Where are you from, Mr. Ross?" Dorothy asked.

"Ottawa," I said.

I felt awkward. It was a mistake to have come.

Mendel drove me to the Château Frontenac.

"Don't forget," he said. "Next time you're here let me know in advance. We'll have you up for dinner."

"You used to tell me jokes, Mendel," I said. "Where did they come from?"

"From the commercial travellers. They come to see me all the time. All of them have jokes. I had one in this morning. What is at the bottom of the sea and shakes?"

"I don't know," I said.

"A nervous wreck," he said and smiled. "Here's another. Why do cows wear bells around their necks?"

I said nothing.

"Because their horns don't work."

He stopped the car outside the entrance of the Château Frontenac.

"When I write to Constance I'll tell her I saw you—"

An hour later I was back in the Viscount taking off from a windswept runway.

THE WHITE SKY

Stephen Scobie

The end will come soon. Within a year, is the prediction.

We have come, the three of us, to this house in the woods, beside the lake, very far away from the city. It took us some time to escape; but I don't think anyone will find us here. After the initial panic, there has been a kind of stunned acceptance; a lot of jobs and businesses continue as usual. But still, there is only a very thin line between these people and chaos. Before the end there will be more violence. The anarchy that tore New York apart will erupt everywhere, until the last choking hours.

We arrived this afternoon, carrying the few supplies we have brought with us. Susan also brought some books, some pens, some paper; I hadn't intended to write again but here I am, the first night, already. As always, that leap into whiteness, putting down the first words on the blank page, trusting in the existence of an audience. But there is no audience now. We have left audiences behind.

Some relics survive of dead civilizations. This may be one.

We walked the last fifty miles or so, having abandoned the jeep, and we destroyed bridges behind us. No-one is likely to follow us, except perhaps Kenneth; and he would find a way, even without bridges.

How shall I describe my feelings, when I blew up that last bridge? We stole the dynamite before we left the city; well, not really "stole," nobody cares any more. You could get almost anything free, once most people realized how useless money had become. I set the charges, carefully, at all the main supports and foundations. It was our last link with the old civilization. No man would ever rebuild this bridge, no man would ever cross this river again. After the blast, there was a secondary explosion of animal life all around; birds squawked and rose, squirrels and rabbits scurried through the bushes. But after a minute, absolute peace descended. Not a sound could be heard. We all felt it, I think, as a forecast of that great silence that will descend before the year is out. Susan was weeping, and Ruth supported her for the next stage of the journey. The bridge was only four black stumps and floating garbage. But the sun was hot overhead and the forest smell was thick around us; light played in all the dappled patterns of forest green. When a bird sang again, I had an absurd moment of hope.

But hope is hopeless. The scientific details are beyond my understanding, as they are beyond most people's, but the situation is clear enough. The atmosphere is sick; the air itself has terminal disease. Incurable. The supply of oxygen is withering. Things will happen at the rate of a geometric progression. Today is twice as bad as yesterday. In the end, say the scientists, there will be a kind of spontaneous combustion, a single flash in which the atmosphere will destroy itself. No life of any kind will survive that moment.

Then, after aeons have passed, some spark of life will stir upon this charred black ball of a planet. The whole thing will start again. The whole thing will start again.

Tonight the moon is very clear beyond the pine trees outside my window. I wish I was on it. I wish I could see, just once, this beautiful planet of mine, a blue and green jewel in a black sky. God, that must be the most wonderful sight. Blue and green, and the great white scuds of cloud around the globe. Shining and pure, the unspoiled Earth. I wish I could see it just one time. I wish I could stand there on the moon's dead surface and look at our living world. Oh God, I wish I could do that just one time. Oh God, God, God, God, God . . . why was so much beauty created, for man to kill it all?

Forgive me. Last night I got very emotional. Anger and

despair and fear and sorrow and frustration—and all that sick, sick feeling we had when first we heard the news.

Today was better. Today I worked in the garden, turning over the soil, planting seeds that may never grow. Just like the baby, now perceptibly swelling in Susan's belly, my baby, our baby, child who may never be born, child whom we conceived a week or so after the news was confirmed. What else can we do? We affirm life, that is all. The soil was thick and rich and moist; it still clings under my fingernails. Ruth brought the seeds: flowers mostly, a few basic vegetables, even a small rose bush. The soft yellow of the Peace rose. Ruth who is herself so beautiful, the long brown hair lying along her shoulders; Susan with her tighter curls, hair cropped around her ears, the pale shining point of the pearl earring I gave her on her birthday, seven years ago. (Seven years ago —could it have been foreseen then? Could it have been prevented?) Today was better, working the soil. For the first time in weeks, the glorious gift of peace was in my heart. I remember the letters I used to receive from Kenneth, who always signed off with the phrase "love and peace." I used to think that pretentious. Not any more. What better things could you wish for a friend, than for him to have love, to love and to be loved, and for him to have peace, peace within himself and his family, peace growing like a calm in the mind? These things you wish for your friends, and for all people, in every thought of them, in every letter, every communication. Kenneth said more in these letters than I did in all my poems. My poems! So worthless now, in all their unproductive anguish. Susan brought a copy of Virgil's *Georgics*—that's the only kind of poetry I would want to write now, with the soil still under my fingernails, and the Peace rose planted close to the lakeshore.

But I do write. Many, many poems. And Susan, when she isn't working, sits by the lakeshore and reads; or else she takes the flute she found in an old cupboard, and plays delicate, reedy melodies. And Ruth is going to paint; she is out in the woods all afternoon, picking various berries to give her colours, mixing them in clay.

Isn't it logical that we turn now to art, the most useless of all human activities, now when nothing is useful anymore? But it gives us great delight. In the evenings we sit around the log fire, and I read new poems and old poems, Susan plays on her flute and Ruth sings sad old ballads in her soft, husky voice. Then we feel so absurdly happy, as the logs burn down and crumple into fine grey feathers.

And we still believe in audiences. Belief, Ruth says, is the last thing to die. Millions of people must still believe in God, thinking that He will step in and save us by a miracle, or else that this is His anger, His punishment, the Second Coming, or something. People believe in God, or in bridges, or in audiences. I write this, as if someone were going to read it. We do all our living "as if" now. Susan and I will have a child, as if he/she could live. We plant seeds, as if they would grow. We paint pictures, as if people might look at them. We live, as if we were not going to die.

We found an iron box. (All sorts of things, we found in this old house.) It may be fireproof. At the end, we shall leave some things in it, which may survive. I think, looking at it, we all had the same brief fantasy: of some explorer from a distant planet, millions of years from now, landing upon this dead, airless world, finding the ruins of man. And only our box, to tell him the whole of human culture. Leonardo forgotten, but Ruth remembered. Scholars of another species attempting to decipher the scrawl of my handwriting!

The fantasy faded, but we kept the box. It is a tangible symbol of our belief in audiences. Life is too wonderful, too various, for it to exist only on this one botched planet. Somewhere life will survive, and do better than we have done. Somewhere a species will learn to control its environment without destroying it—will learn, that is, to control itself. It must be so.

Our other "audience" is, of course, Susan's baby. Six-month foetus, crouched and fishlike in the dark still womb, our faded future, will you ever be born? Will you ever breathe our air, before our air can no longer be breathed? Ever see the light, before there is no light to see?

Will you in your pre-natal silence understand my words?

I was your father. I was known as a poet; I wrote under a pseudonym, and many people knew me by that name. Few people knew me by my private name; but one of these was Susan. Susan was your mother. (We were never married.) Susan played music on the flute; she sat beside the logfire, waiting as the months went by, and you in her belly ripened like a fruit in summer, while the world waned deathwards like a cold moon. I loved your mother. Love was the element in which you grew. There was no fear in your conception. There were several nights of joy, in my bare rooms, while fires flickered in the city all around us. That week, the week of your conception, there were many suicides. Many people chose to die. Others chose to live by their fear, and some by their hatred, released now by a total lack of repressions. Law became a mockery. How can you sentence to death a dying man? Or say "Ten years in prison"? There were fires in all the cities of the earth, that night you were conceived. Some people chose to live by love. We chose to create you, out of love, out of the affirmation of life, the only gesture left to us. Ruth also loves. Ruth loves her husband Kenneth, who has promised to join us later. Kenneth is a scientist; he is one of many working round the clock to try and find some solution. They all know it is too late. They have all the resources of the world to command, and they know it is too late. Kenneth will work out of a sense of duty. If there is even the faintest possibility of hope, he will work. But when the end comes near, he will come to us, if he can. Ruth waits for that. When Kenneth comes, we will know that the end is very close. Kenneth is my brother, your uncle. He also loves you. Child, you have so much love surrounding you. All the love our lives can contain is directed towards you now. I long to see you. I long to see you before I die, my son, my daughter, child of my blood, and hers whom I love. The candle is sputtering low. I should write more in the daytime; we don't have very many candles. Ruth is asleep. Susan is in bed, but will not sleep till I come. The candle has gone out, and I strain to see as I write these last few words in the dim moonlight.

I should be able to describe this place—(I'm supposed to be a poet)—I should be able to create it again in my words. How that arrowhead of land juts out into the lake, with pine trees like a row of skittles collapsing into the mist . . . . Mixed metaphors, skittles on an arrowhead. A narrow point of land; a row of trees; the last tree is bent out over the water. There is usually a mist around dawn, until the sun dispels it, a low, white mist. They say that when the end comes, the sky will turn white. For several hours, the sky will be absolutely white. And then a single flash of fire. Death will be instantaneous. Nobody will suffer any pain. The sky will turn white.

I should be able to describe this place, I'm supposed to be a poet. But my poems were never like that. I didn't write descriptive poems. I created fantastic landscapes of the mind, and peopled them with phantoms and tormentors. I wrote poems about an anguish which I didn't really feel, even then. I see now that they were all dishonest poems. Many critics praised them. Many people read them, people whose souls were truly anguished, or people who wanted to know what it felt like. My poems were peep-shows of imagined nightmare. They were dishonest poems, I see that now. They were dishonest to my own experience, but more than that, they were dishonest to poetry. I have perhaps become dogmatic, but I say this now—poems like that are unjustifiable, aesthetically. Poetry is not a mirror for self-indulgence, is not an acid bubble-bath for self-pity to wallow in. I used to write poems about mangled birds; I never wrote poems about the whole bird on the tree. It isn't easy. A very great poet once said, "I think the poets must bear the anguish of not writing anguish poems." I have been trying, now, to write poems that are, quite simply, the celebration of life. We affirm life, that is all we can do. I look now in my psyche for these dark places which ancient explorers would label "Here be dragons." I find none. The poems I am writing now are poor poems, because I haven't yet mastered the craft. Perhaps I never will. But they are poems. And it isn't easy. Despair is so easy. Despair is just around every corner of my mind—but it has no place there. It is alien. Poetry is the celebration.

158

Poetry is love and peace, the gentle yellow of that rose. And we are all so calm here! Such a deep inner peace is descending on us! Susan daily folds in on herself like a flower, centred on that growth within her. Ruth has begun painting, with home-made brush and paints. She sits by the lake, waiting for Kenneth. Sometimes I catch her voice singing; sometimes Susan plays her flute and the birds respond. I work in the soil, extending our garden. Next year (if there was a next year) we could be fully self-supporting. We need a cow to give us milk. I have planted out the vegetables, lettuce and cauliflower and broccoli, potatoes. I cut wood for the fire, using fallen dead trees; if possible, I don't cut anything living. I clear the jumble of withered bushes so that new plants can grow underneath. The same with my poems. I am clearing away dead matter, encouraging new growth. I sit and wrestle with words and rhythms that will not come. It is frustrating, I suppose, in some ways; but I am content. Perhaps, before the end, I shall have written a few poems worth preserving, a few pages to put in that iron box that will probably not survive, nor ever be opened. Not the poems of anguish; and not pseudonymous either. I will sign them with my private name.

Waiting. We are all waiting, that is the essential characteristic of our lives now. Waiting for the end, but waiting also for more immediate things. I wait for a rose to bloom, for a plant to break the soil's surface, for a poem to click into place. Susan waits for her child; Ruth waits for her husband.

It was Ruth who was saying all this, today, this afternoon. I was sitting on a rock at the edge of the lake, with my notebook open. Several attempts at poems were scored out; I should really be more careful with paper, we don't have an unlimited supply. I had been writing, but then I was just sitting, half-asleep in the sun. Ruth came swimming by, and climbed up on the rock beside me, naked, the water gleaming on her flesh in the sunlight. (Embarrassment or modesty about our bodies scarcely seem important now; absurd, rather.) We talked. It's not often that we talk directly about the end—that's not because we're afraid, none of us is afraid, but simply because we haven't anything new to say about it—but today, Ruth talked about waiting.

"You know all these people," she said, "who offer glib definitions of man as 'the animal who . . . '; you know, 'the animal who laughs,' 'the animal who remembers,' 'the animal who suffers guilt,' and so on. Mine is simpler than any of these. Man is the animal who waits."

"Waiting is a rather passive quality," I suggested, "to be the characteristic of a creature so energetic that he has destroyed his whole planet."

"No, waiting isn't passive," she replied. "You wait *for* something, even if it's only for death. To wait, you have to know that something is coming, you must have awareness. Then you set your mind to it. That gives you a purpose."

"I've always thought of waiting as a rather empty activity," I confessed. "Like those tramps in *Waiting for Godot*."

"Oh no. They're not empty. They're fulfilled. They've found a purpose; if necessary, they've created one. Look—like us now. We're all waiting for the end, right? For the morning of the white sky. And that's certain, we know it will come, and we know roughly when. So we train ourselves to that end. We adopt a certain attitude. What's the phrase from *Hamlet*? 'The readiness is all.' OK. That's great. But this as well—I'm waiting for Kenneth. I love him. My whole body is waiting for him. But it's uncertain. I don't know when he's coming. I don't know if he *is* coming. He may be dead. He may never make it in time. I may die without ever seeing him again. But I wait for him anyway. And if he was here, I would wait for something else."

"Eh?"

"People always wait for something else. They're never satisfied with what they've got. If they walk they want a car. If they've got a car, they want two. Give them enough cars and they'll want a plane. Give them a planet and they'll want its moon as well. You always hope for one thing more than you've got, because ultimately you've got 70 years or so of life and you want eternity. You want it all the time you're waiting for death."

"Why do you paint, Ruth?"

She laughed. "Because I'm waiting for a painting that will reach out and pull me into it and hide me inside the canvas forever."

"That way you would have eternity?"

"I suppose so."

"And what would you wait for then?"

"Nothing," she said. "I wouldn't be human any more. Like that poem by Yeats—

> Once out of nature I shall never take
> My bodily form from any natural thing,
> But such a form as Grecian goldsmiths make . . . .

Isn't that why you write poems?"

"Since we're indulging in so many literary allusions," I replied, "I'll give you one more. I'm waiting for my words to reach, after speech, into the silence."

"Silence at least we shall have soon enough," she said, sitting up. And her breasts moved, with the last droplets of water shining below them; her body, tanning a deep brown in the sun of our last summer, seemed so beautiful to me that again the old bitter thought flashed through my mind, oh God, why was so much beauty created, for man to kill it all? But bitterness is something we have left behind, thank God. We don't have time to be bitter, now—did we ever? My thought remained, without the bitterness. I remembered Kenneth, who signed his letters "Love and peace," even his business letters, even his payments of bills. I said to her, "I hope he makes it."

She smiled, then slid back into the water. The squished-up image of her body, seeming pale now in the water, flickered down. She swam along the shoreline in long, easy strokes. There was grace and precision in her movements, the grace of a perfect form. Like the stillness of a painting, or music, or sometimes (with so much difficulty) words. I realized that our lives also were becoming like that, the three of us. Almost impersonal, our individualities fading into the unified action of our life. In calmness and stillness we are becoming such a form; the gap between life and art is closing; we are a poem.

161

Do you understand me? (Strange question, reader; unknown, non-existent you.) I wish I could say it better. I wish the words would come. Is it like this in the cities? Are people there also experiencing this calm, this unity, this enriching of their lives? Or is it implicit in our isolation, in our direct contact with the soil and the water, in the aesthetic form of the gesture we have made? Would people in the cities now understand me? Or is the failure in my words, in my clumsy attempts to communicate a feeling so subtle and yet so strong? Perhaps better words will come, in time. Perhaps. That at least is something I can wait for.

And Susan waits, for our child to be born. She has changed a lot. In those days when we first knew and loved each other . . . . I was about to write "the old, carefree days," but what a farcical word that would have been! Here, we are free from cares in a way we never were then, even though we lived without a shadow over us, from day to day; two people, fairly young, fairly rich, reading books and going to parties, smiling on the outskirts of political discussions, then going home to bed. We followed the fashions, and wrote articles for influential magazines. We took holidays in Europe, and were meditating Japan for this summer. Instead, our luxury hotel is this old wooden house, built by some rich man a hundred years ago beside a lake, with hundreds of miles in every direction of forest, mountain, river, lake, valley, wilderness. Instead, Susan sits daily in the sun, reading, or playing her flute; but these are secondary occupations; primarily, Susan is pregnant, and she bends over the child with an intense love, as if she were trying to communicate to the unborn (and perhaps never to be born) child, to the child simultaneously growing and dying, all the peace, all the love, all the beauty of being human, of which the child will never become conscious.

It was Susan who suggested the idea. For a week after the official confirmation of the rumours which leapt wildly around the cities (the government had tried to keep it secret, but to no avail), for a week the panic raged, there were lootings and murders, all restraints were gone, it appeared as if the end were going to be a very dreadful thing. It is still strange to me that things have calmed down at all, though the peace when we left the city was a very uneasy one. In that first week we hid in Susan's apartment, but when the mobs came closer we retreated to mine. It had already been looted. When we had cleaned up the wreckage, the rooms were almost bare. The electricity didn't work, but we had light from the fires burning in several sections of the city. Then it was Susan who suggested that we might attempt to come here to live out the last few months. Her family used to own the house, but it hadn't been used for years. I agreed; I thought it was a splendid idea. Then Susan said, "And another thing. Let's have a baby."

I wonder, sometimes, how many other people had the same idea. In that time of violence, rape was not uncommon; many children must have been conceived. But how many people deliberately chose to create a new life which they knew could never survive? We cannot even be sure that the baby will ever be born. Kenneth said that a year was an optimistic guess; he himself estimated six months. We knew that. And we have no medical facilities here; Ruth has some training, but not much; the birth will be painful, and Susan may die. Or the child may die. But we will all die anyway. It doesn't matter; it just doesn't matter. It is, in a sense, a very selfish thing. We want the child for our own gratification, so that *we* can feel that *we* have done something, have made some kind of gesture, the affirmation of life. The love that surrounds this child means more to us than it ever will to him, or her. And this also we have accepted, and are not ashamed of. We live *as if* there were a future, *as if* our love would someday focus on an individual human being, rather than on that almost abstract concept, "the child." The child grows in Susan's belly, which swells like the changing moon. It's a beautiful sight. I come from the garden, my hands still dirty with the good earth, and kiss Susan, and feel with my hands the centre of the growing life. And I kneel beside her in the warm sun as she reaches for her flute and sends her delicate melody into the air. The Peace rose is in bloom.

Kenneth arrived last night. We had all gone out of the house to watch the moon rise over the highest tips of the pine trees, whose shapes were outlined in absolute black against the silver light. The moon was full, and we all stood silently, caught in its beauty. How many more full moons would we see? Then Ruth cried out that something was moving behind the house. I went round, and heard a stumbling sound in the bushes beside the path. I called out, "Who's there?" and a man's figure rose, lifted an arm, then fell flat forward on his face. I ran up to him. It was Kenneth. He was badly wounded.

We carried him into the house and stripped away his filthy clothes. Ruth was crying. God knows how he ever made it, in his condition, such a distance. Later, when he recovered consciousness, he told us his story. Violence had broken out again, sheer panic, directed this time against the government and against the scientists. They had to blame someone. It had become increasingly clear that nothing could be done, that the research being done so frantically by Kenneth and thousands of others was ten or fifteen years too late. Kenneth sensed the growing desperation and hostility at the daily press conferences. At last the mobs broke loose again, and attacked the research centres. Many were killed. Kenneth himself was captured by the mobs and held as their prisoner for several days. Finally he attempted to escape, failed, and was brutally punished. He tried again, and this time he got away, though a guard's rifle put a bullet through his shoulder. Then began his incredible journey to join us, hundreds of miles to the north. He stole a jeep, which he used till it ran out of fuel, then walked. He came to the bridge I had blown up, and somehow, despite his shoulder, he crossed the river. Then he got lost and wandered in circles for four days till he climbed a mountain and got his bearings. From there it was two more days. But he made it.

Ruth nursed him, dressing his wounds, sitting beside him all night. She was magnificently happy. She had what she was waiting for. We left them alone, but I don't think they spoke much. He clasped her hand and she smiled happily into his eyes. My brother and her husband;

164

he had made it. Something was completed now, something was accomplished. The unity was perfected. Susan and I slept in the next room; all four of us were together.

Kenneth arrived last night, and this morning he died. We buried him beside the lake, with the white mists rising and curling round the feet of the tall black pines. I dug his grave and heaped the good earth on top of it; we returned his body to the dying ground. And we were not sad; we did not mourn for him. There was no weeping at his burial. He made it. Across a thousand miles of wilderness, with wounds that should have killed him long before, he made it. He made it back to Ruth, to the woman he loved, and he died in her arms so quietly, so happily, like a child falling to sleep. We stood round his grave as the mists rose from the calm surface of the lake, and Ruth laid on the mound the first flower of the yellow rose. Love and peace, brother. Something is completed; the unity is perfect. Lake and sky were blue as we moved away from the grave, and Susan played a soft, slow song. All four of us were together. Kenneth arrived last night.

And with Kenneth's arrival, things began to grow more fully. The rose blossomed in profusion; the flower-beds burst into colour; we began to harvest our own vegetables at last, and stopped relying on the stocks of canned food. Ruth began to paint the flowers. She had two distinct styles of painting, between which she alternated: one, meticulously detailed and accurate reproductions, botanical drawings; the other, bright, impressionistic splotches of colour. Her paintings became more joyful, more exuberant even than before. (But I knew she had painted, although she never showed them to us, a painting of Kenneth as he lay on her bed that night, and several quiet sketches of the grave by the shore of the lake.) Susan sat with her often. And I have been writing again; at last, the kind of poems I wanted to write. They are not directly about our life here—that was my mistake, to try that—they are, I suppose you would call them fantasies, though I don't think of them as fantasies in the sense of impossible stories, because they are possible. They are fantasies of life as it used to be, informed with the knowledge, with the love and peace we now possess. They try to imagine a life where people could live this way naturally, not because the end is so close; they are projections of our present personalities into what is now a fictional setting. In one sense, they are a requiem for Kenneth; but they aren't sad. They're not anguish poems. They are simple, constructive things—like the bridge we built.

More than a month had passed since Kenneth's arrival. Almost daily now, we expected the end. He had said, that night, that we wouldn't see many leaves change colour. Susan's baby is also very close to birth. Ruth went exploring along the shore behind the house. She found old paths which lead through the forests, until they come to a swift, rocky stream that pours down into the lake. There was an old wooden, broken-down bridge across the stream. Beyond it, about half a mile or so, is a large patch of wild brambles. There's a glade in the woods, which is cool even in the heat of the day. It was obviously a favourite spot of the people who originally built the house.

Ruth took me there, and we waded across the stream beside the broken bridge. "Why don't you fix it?" she said. "You destroyed bridges on your way here; now's the time to make amends."

"You have a thing about bridges," I replied, climbing up on the bank to have a look at it.

"It's a secular idea," she laughed. "If you don't have faith in God, have faith in bridges. Especially suspension bridges."

I took a close look at what needed to be done. The basic structure and supports of the bridge seemed sound; it was the actual deck that had rotted and broken away. I would need to make about a dozen stout planks, and somehow fasten them down. (We had no nails.) In fact, I would probably need to cut down a tree. But it could be done.

Ruth was enthusiastic; so was Susan. So we all set out, with a hefty old axe Ruth had found in the attic, and a small handsaw we had brought with us, which I had used for preparing firewood. Quite absurdly inadequate tools!

But we managed all right. I whacked away at the tree in my best movie lumberjack style; Ruth had a few swings too; and after an unscientific hour or so, it fell, to enthusiastic cries of "Timber!" from all three of us. Then we spent laborious hours sawing the trunk; I sharpened the saw as best I could on some rocks which looked vaguely like flint. Making the planks took about two days; while I sawed away, Ruth collected all kinds of long grasses and reeds, and Susan sat braiding them into rope. This was an even slower business than carving the planks; but at last Ruth and I carried the planks down to the bridge, cut away the old ones, and fitted the new into place, binding them down as securely as we could with the rope.

It was scarcely a professional job; I seem to be better at blowing bridges up than I am at repairing them. But it would hold, for the very short time left. Ruth paraded across first, with a broad grin, to the music of Susan's flute; and then Susan herself followed (crossing the stream for the first time) and we all went to sit in the cool green glade.

There we sat throughout the afternoon. Susan began talking, saying how close to the end we must be (unusual, for, as I have written, we rarely talk about it directly) and as we listened she suddenly suggested that, before the end, Ruth and I should make love together. We were both surprised and a bit puzzled; then Susan leant forward and said in an intense voice, "But don't you see, it may be *the last time.*" At once we were struck, simultaneously, by the absurdity and the awesomeness of the idea. Since Kenneth's return, we have discounted the cities in our thinking. They may be calm again, or more likely they will have degenerated into total anarchy. With sublime egotism, we have, almost consciously, assumed that we are the last people on Earth to live without fear, in peace and love. In all its history, the human race has found one act (the most common of all actions, the act we share with every living species) in which its capacity for love (and also, of course, for hate) has been focussed: the union of man and woman in an ecstasy which is both our most personal and our most impersonal act. Now, Susan was saying, now this also is ending. Now for the last time will

167

two people move to meet each other in this way. And the last time must not be a moment of fear or hate, of rape or terror; it must be a moment of love. And Susan is pregnant and Kenneth is dead. So Ruth and I face each other in the green light of the forest, uncertain whether to weep or to laugh out loud. We sat in silence, aware enough of the moment's absurdity to meditate giggling, aware enough of its solemnity to keep the silence. Until Ruth stretched out her hand to me, and I took it, feeling her fingers cool in my palm.

But it was several days before we came together, quietly one night when she came to my room. That duality of feeling, awe and absurdity, persisted even then. At first I felt as if I were part of a ritual, as if all the generations of men, and all those never to be born, moved with me in the act; but later, we lay together and laughed at the pretentiousness of our thoughts. And since then, we have slept together each night, and our lovemaking has become more natural, no longer so loaded with "significance." And that, of course, is how the last time should be—neither awesome nor absurd, simply the love that we make, every day, in our lives together.

I began to clear new land for further planting next spring. I cleared a tangle of underbrush from a patch of ground about 150 feet square, and we burnt it in a magnificent bonfire. Then I spent several very hard days digging out the roots, attacking them with the axe. There were also some large boulders, which Ruth and I contrived to roll away, and a lot of smaller rocks to be carried. Then I dug the whole thing over, and more or less started again on clearing out more roots and stones. The soil was good, black and fertile; I could see that there would be some drainage problems, so I planned out a system of ditches and began to dig them. Ruth helped me with most of this work, but we never strayed out of earshot of the house; and indeed it was while we were up there, late in a hot afternoon, that we heard Susan's first calls.

The labour was long and painful. I felt sick, and escaped for walks along the lakeshore. Ruth of course stayed with her all the time. At last, sometime about an hour before dawn, the child was born. It was a boy, fine and healthy. When I came into the room, Susan was lying still in the bed, so absolutely pale and motionless that for a moment I thought she was dead. There was such an absolute contrast between the whiteness of her face and the boy's scrunched-up red. He seemed so tiny and fragile. Then Susan turned her head and smiled at me; I sat on the side of the bed, unable to stand up. Ruth was leaning against the wall in utter weariness. The baby started crying.

We held a simple naming ceremony the next day. We called him, of course, Kenneth. Susan was very weak for several days, but she nursed him herself; Ruth looked after him the rest of the time. I felt a strange embarrassment in their presence; I am clumsy when handling small things, and I was very nervous about holding the child. I worked a lot, out in the new patch of ground. The drainage system has been worked out far more elaborately than necessary. Ruth came out a couple of times to help me; and three nights after the birth she came to my bed again. After about a week, Susan was better, strong again, and we all felt more at ease.

I carved a cradle out of a fallen log, and here the boy slept, in Susan's room. More than ever our life has become centred around him. Watching over him, we have felt stirrings of old angers; we have been so perfect here, so fulfilled, that we have long ceased to be angry for ourselves —but that he, Kenneth, should so soon be deprived of every chance to experience life, to know and love as we have loved and known, arouses in us those feelings of rage and frustration and grief that we first experienced all these months ago. But it was then that we decided to create this one new life; and the life is here. To see him, held in Susan's arm as he sucks the milk from her breast, is all the answer we need. Everything for which we waited has come to pass.

And now there are hints of autumn in the air. Now the morning air is chillier, and the mist on the surface of the lake persists longer before the sun can dispel it. Now the Peace rose shows no new buds; on some of the trees, touches of brown are curling up the tips of the leaves. The earth is turning, tipping this northern hemisphere away from the sun. The nights grow longer.

It is finished. Ruth woke me in the middle of the night; there was a flickering light in the sky. We got out of bed and went through to wake Susan. All night we watched: flashes and flickers of light darting across the whole sky, like lightning, but more constant, of a greater intensity, and all in frightening silence.

Then, this morning, when the sun rose, the sky was white. All, absolutely white, like a page upon which no word has been written. And silence all around, so that we speak in whispers.

So, I have put our records in this flimsy iron box: my poems, Ruth's paintings, Susan's flute, and finally this diary, which I close now. I will go down to the lakeshore to join the others. Susan is feeding her baby; Ruth is crouched by the shore, letting the lake water run through her fingers. The white sky casts no shadows.

Love and peace.

DON BAILEY was born in Toronto in 1942. He dropped out of school in Grade 11, but went back several times and finally finished. He has spent five years in prison, lives in Toronto, but has travelled in Canada a lot and plans to do more. He works at the Christian Resource Centre. A selection of his poems appeared in *Soundings*.

GWENDOLYN MACEWEN was born in Toronto in 1941. She left school at eighteen to write. She has four books of poetry and two novels, most recently *The Twelve Circles of the Night*. In 1969 she won the Governor General's Award for poetry. At the moment she is especially interested in the study of languages, notably Arabic.

HUGH GARNER was born in 1913 in Batley, Yorkshire. He was educated in Toronto schools and left Danforth Tech after Grade 10. He has lived mostly in Toronto and is the author of ten books of fiction. The most recent are *The Sin Sniper* and *A Nice Place to Visit*. He is now completing his fourth collection of stories.

NORA KEELING was born in Owen Sound on Christmas Day, 1933. She has studied at the University of Western Ontario and the Royal Academy of Dramatic Art, where she was a contemporary of Albert Finney. She lived in France for several years and has recently taught French at Western. She is working on a book of stories.

KENT THOMPSON was born in Waukegan, Illinois in 1936. He was educated in the United States and at the University of Wales at Swansea, but has now lived longer in Fredericton, where he teaches at UNB, than anywhere else. He has published a chapbook of poetry, *Hard Explanations*, and has written comedy and commentary for the CBC in Fredericton and Halifax. He is now working on a play and a novel.

D.O. SPETTIGUE was born in London, Ontario in 1930. He has degrees from Western and Toronto. He has spent most of his life in southern Ontario. A group of his stories was included in *New Canadian Writing: 1969* and he is the author of a book on the RCMP and a controversial study of the life and work of Frederick Philip Grove. He is spending the academic year 1971–72 in Europe, on sabbatical leave from Queen's University, where he teaches English.

PHYLLIS GOTLIEB was born in Toronto in 1926. She has an MA from the University of Toronto and three children.She is the author of two novels and two books of poetry. In 1969 she published a novel, *Why Should I Have All the Grief*, and a book of poems, *Ordinary, Moving*. She has just finished a new novel.

171